Agnes Mary Frances Robinson

Arden - A Novel

Vol. II

Agnes Mary Frances Robinson

Arden - A Novel
Vol. II

ISBN/EAN: 9783337032395

Printed in Europe, USA, Canada, Australia, Japan

Cover: Foto ©Andreas Hilbeck / pixelio.de

More available books at **www.hansebooks.com**

ARDEN

A NOVEL

BY

A. MARY F. ROBINSON

IN TWO VOLUMES

VOL II.

LONDON
LONGMANS, GREEN, AND CO.
1883

CONTENTS

OF

THE SECOND VOLUME.

— ⚫◆⚫ —

ARDEN.

CHAPTER XIII.

EYES AND NO EYES.

ARDEN began her picture, and talked and thought of little else by day, and dreamed of it by night. It was not, you see, merely a work of art; it was a future, or rather the possible resurrection of her past. The canvas, representing a brilliant appleyard full of crimson and yellow fruit, floored with vivid aftermath, shot and streaked with sunlight, was be sent to Birmingham Exhibition, was, of course, to be accepted, to be sold for fifty pounds, and to fetch in many even higher-priced commissions.

Then she would go back to Rome ; Arden
sometimes thought, and always dreamed,
that she would find her father there, and
indeed without him she could not even
imagine Rome. His sudden loss had had
a strange effect upon her, one only possible
in a person tenacious in affection, dense of
perception, subject to an unimaginative,
practical,   but   all-pervading   dreaminess.
Since she came to England she had never
felt the keen despair that most girls would
have felt in her situation ; life did not
seem in the least over for her ; on the
other hand, she was roused to an im-
patience, an activity quite foreign to her
disposition, by an odd, unformulated conviction that her father, her happiness, her
home, were being hidden from her ; were,
not lost, but secreted in some unknown
place which it was not hopeless to discover.
She had the superstitious clinging to the
lost, which makes religious people spend
half their lives in a Paradise, where all

that has been taken from them remains unchanged by death. Arden, who could not realise a future different to the past, who yearned so passionately for the present, fancied Paradise an invention of the early Tuscan painters for the sake of charmingly contrasted pictorial effects ; yet she had something of the same idea, but applied it differently. With her, too, the bitterness of death was robbed of its sting, the cruel realisation of hopeless, irremediable, eternal loss. Arden, too, had her Paradise.

Was it so very strange ? Are many beliefs, for which martyrs have died, which in their turn have sacrificed an army of martyrs, are the great beliefs of the world so much better founded, so much more capable of being reasoned, so much firmer on a clearly-posed logical basis, than this superstition, born of dim anxious yearning, of refusal to accept the worst, this immortalisation of memory in the mind of a young and dreamy woman ?

Meanwhile, the working at her picture brought her into constant contact with the people at the Farm. Gradually she became aware that, apart from the satisfaction of painting, there was a certain pleasure in going to the Williams's. They were always so glad to see her. There was no doubt that after the constrained, burdened, silent life of the Bushes it was pleasant to listen to Susie's eager determined theories as she sat by Arden's side in the sun-shot orchard, her chin propped in her palm, appealing, indignant, throwing her whole heart into every question, moral, social, artistic ; always turning her words into opinions, her opinions into theories, her theories into combats, and in the strength and militance of her decision, ignoring the semi-accidental cause of it.

Perhaps, after all, the great charm was that this resolute, convinced young theorist paid Arden every homage that respect, affection, sympathy could suggest. Arden had seen so much, could talk about Rome, Pompeii, Syracuse, Florence, as Harry talked of Raynham and Faversham; she could answer so many questions, solve so many doubts, confirm so many suppositions. Moreover, she was beautiful, delicate, refined, an orphan. To Susie's ardent and chivalrous temperament each of these qualities was alone a reason for devoted attachment. Arden, therefore, always found herself treated as the supreme court of appeal by a pleader of character and intellect far stronger than her own. Lonely, weak, neglected, she was not insensible to the flattery. The brother also interested her, though she saw but little of him. Probably, had she known him better, she would have cared less. As it was, the constant half-allusions, unsaid praises, profound admiration of Harry in Susie's conversation, was not without effect. She remembered that on her first interview with him he had impressed her as a person of much kindness and energy. She was glad little Susie had so excellent a brother, and when she looked at the swampy or arid fields and the unkempt drive of the Bushes she contrasted them, in her own mind, with Harry Williams's management of his affairs.

So without any active interest, always with the feeling that this acquaintance was merely a stop-gap, she grew accustomed to find the Williams's a familiar part of her surrounding world. While she was painting her picture and dreaming of the future she gave a facile, half-attention to Susie's eager kindness, to her mother's well-meant fussinesses ; and though she set them down as nothing, they sank deeper than she knew ; for, at this time, the only three people in the world who seemed to care much if she coughed or sang, if she sighed or laughed, waked or slept, all lived at Woodleigh Farm.

It was strange, perhaps, that after such a different society Arden should be satisfied with simple farmers. But she never dreamed of seeking their society. She went to the Farm to paint, never for any other reason; she herself was unaware how much real friendliness the kindness and interest of these rustic people had awakened for them in her heart. At present she still ostensibly regarded them as the proprietors of the orchard.

One day Mrs. Lawrance, seeing Arden take up her hat and leave the parlour, followed her to the hall door.

' So you're aäf again to Williams's ? '

' Yes ; to my picture.'

' You're allus arter that girl, now.'

' Oh no, Mrs. Lawrance ; I don't see her even, sometimes. I'm only painting the orchard.'

'And when will you a-done with it—
th' archard ?'

'It depends a good deal on the weather.
If this sort of weather goes on, not till the
end of the month.'

'Ay, ay; you're allus puling and
pining, Sylvie; fretting or frabbing at
summut. If you was less ignorant you'ld
ha' perceived the turnips was at last ex-
tremities for want of rain.'

'Very likely. Italian turnips are more
to my taste ; they get their rain and their
disagreeableness all in a lump.'

'Ah! 'Tis a pity you ever left your
Italians!'

'Indeed, yes. But let me sell my
picture, and then to damp skies and
England, *Buonanotte* !'

Arden ran down the drive, letting fly
the last sentence. She was sufficiently
cross to feel a certain satisfaction in
imagining how ungrateful and unkind
her last words would seem to Mrs.

Lawrance. But nothing was too hard
for such a cross-grained old woman. Her
grandfather she really liked and cared for
—but Mrs. Lawrance! Arden's dislike
was perhaps sharpened by the suspicion
that Mrs. Lawrance possessed more
strength of feeling and capacity for fine
action than all the true Lawrances together.
Superior qualities are exasperating in a
person one detests. By this time the girl was
at the drive-gate. Her passion was cooled,
and she felt a little repentant, but the sense
of being in the way made her still more
anxious to get away from this England
of lush boggy greenness, of spongy outlines, thick air, untremulous and dull,
skies without atmosphere, summers without glory or prostration, where she was
always cross, fatigued, and in the wrong.
Oh, she did not see the moment of getting
away!

As she mused thus, leaning her arms on
the high gate and her head on her arms,

she looked idly down the lane towards the bridge.

'Miss Lawrance,' cried a fresh provincial voice from the side. It was Susie, walking briskly, a little basket on her arm.

'I've been to the Boltons',' she explained, 'for we ran out of yeast. I thought I should find you at home— aren't you going to paint to-day, Miss Lawrance?'

'Paint! Oh yes—everything depends on that!'

'May I walk with you down the lane?'

'I shall be glad.'

The two girls started off together; Arden's slim figure, uncertain pace, charm of movement, contrasting with the rustic steadiness and straightness of her companion.

Susie looked up. 'We shall have wind,' she cried.

Then she picked a flower at her feet. 'And rain, I fear,' she added.

' Oh, I hope not!' said Arden.

' I hope not too; the corn's scarce turning yet in the shady fields ; but there's marestails in the sky over yon, Miss Lawrance, to the windward, and see this pimpernel's closing before noon.'

' Dear me!' cried Arden, ' I shouldn't think it meant anything. What are marestails? Oh, those swathes of clouds? And that little red flower—is that your barometer?'

' You see it's so delicate, it shuts up at the damp air, just as the slug, there, comes out when he sniffs the rain.'

' Ugly little bestia!' Arden moved out of its way.

' Oh, Miss Lawrance!' Susie stooped down. ' I think he's so pretty. See, his shoulders are covered with a pattern, just like the carter's smock-frocks ! '

' Still, I don't think he's pretty.'

They went on a little longer, Susie
keeping close to the hedges and ditches.

'I'm looking for an orchid; I found one
here once and never again—all green. I've
got one pressed; but I never found
another.'

'But what good would it be? A green
thing's not pretty to look at, like a rose.'

'I've got a book at home,' said Susie,
'where I've pressed 'most every kind of
flower to be found in these parts. You
wouldn't believe what a many there are!
Hundreds!'

'You should see the flowers in Italy!'

'If I could! Oh, there's more than
flowers I want of Italy—books, pictures,
history—things I can't have here. Still,
there's a many good things in Arden, more
than you know, Miss Lawrance.' She
looked half-shrewdly, half-sweetly at Arden,
as if she wished the girl to understand a
liking she would not speak of; but in a
moment she was off, her hands above her

head, a Caryatide in cotton, searching among
the tiny green plants and fern that grew in
the damp interstices of the bricks of the
bridge.

'Here!' she cried, 'look, Miss Lawrance, isn't it a lovely little fern? I've
never found it before ; but Mrs. Grubb, at
the post-office (she's great in flowers, you
know), she told me as sometimes it sprang
here!'

Her eyes and one arm were still high
up the wall, but, half-turning, she lowered
the hand which held the tiny plant.

' Isn't it beautiful?' she asked.

' I think it's rather like the others,' said
Arden. ' They're all alike, *Felce* ; not much
good except for doing up in bouquets.'

Susie's face fell a little. She privately
thought it a little dull of Arden not to feel
an interest in her plant; but her instincts
of hero-worship immediately suggested
that Arden, who had seen the greatest
things of the world, could scarcely be

expected to care for such very small ones. Still, she kept her plant, tying it carefully in her handkerchief.

'How still it is, and the sun so bright and yellow! There's a storm brewing.'

'How do you know?'

'Those are all signs. Hark! how loud the birds sing. D'ye hear? Yon's a black-bird. Fancy, at this season!'

'Do you know the birds by their voices?'

'Oh, yes, all of them. See, the swallows are gathering; I saw a Fare-thee-well-summer yesterday.'

'What's that?'

'A flower. It only comes when the swallows gather and the good weather's done.'

'Done! It seems to me we have never had any.'

'Oh Missie! Six fine days last week for the corn, and rain before and after for the roots; a spell of sunshine now, and we should have never such a harvest.'

'I don't care for the turnips; I care for the sun.'

Arden was not in a conciliatory mood: Susie perceived it.

'Of course you miss your home,' she said; 'you see, this is my home. I've always lived here—I've never known anything better. I would rather live here than anywhere in the world!'

'Is it possible!' cried Arden.

She began pouring out an incoherent eulogy of all the items that made up the world in which she had been happy—fitful-coloured olive-hills, white villas guarded by pointing cypresses, the great plain of the Campagna, the grey and lilac ridges of the Sabine range. Suddenly she stopped.

'There is the postman. Let us walk a little quicker.'

'Do you expect a letter?'

'Yes ; from the Roses : from my old friends, from the people who would take me away.'

'Take you away! Would you be so glad to go?'

Arden, for all her hurry, stopped a moment ; stopped with brilliant eyes and flushed cheeks, suddenly clouded with hesitation. Would she be glad to go? It was a question she had never asked herself. It seemed so sensible, so self-evident and necessary that she must be glad to go. What was there here she could regret to leave? What was there over there she did not long to look upon again?

Before she could put this thought into words, Susie, seizing her opportunity, had begun to speak.

'See, Miss Lawrance,' she began, ' I know you've had much to make you wretched-like since you've been among us. You came unhappy to a new place where the people of your own rank haven't been over-good to you, or hospitable at all.'

Arden blushed.

'I beg your pardon for speaking of it, Miss Lawrance, but plain words are best. And the old gentleman's been ill; you must have had a dull, lonely life of it up at the Bushes—no blame to them.'

Susie stopped a moment, but seeing the postman coming nearer and nearer she hurried on.

'You've had no one but us to know—farmer-people, and quite out of your station. See, Miss Lawrance, I understand why you should be glad to go. I didn't think of it before; but of course you looked on us much as you looked on th' 'emlock and th' apple-trees as you painted.'

'Oh, no!' said Arden, growing redder; but she felt it to be true.

'It was natural,' went on Susie, sadly, 'but all the time I've been thinking of you, and caring for you with real love.—

Don't speak, there's no need you should say anything—and if your friends call for you, go, dear Miss Lawrance, and be happier than you've been here. But if you stay——'

The girl stopped a moment to swallow something.

'Dear Susie!' whispered Arden, and took the girl's hand.

'If you stay,' went on the other, keeping hold of the little hand, ' there's something I have it on my mind to tell you. God knows I've no call to preach. But this isn't preaching, Miss Lawrance, it's only showing you something, as I showed you the little fern—and you needn't heed it any more than that, unless you like.'

'Go on,' said Arden.

' Well, Miss Lawrance, you don't like the country here; but you see to-day when the blackbird sang you didn't recognise it and scarcely heard it. You didn't see any meaning in the sky; you didn't understand what it meant when the beasts crowded under the trees, and the birds sang so loud, and the sunshine looked so yellow; you didn't know one flower from another, and scarcely saw a difference between them—now, did you, Miss Lawrance?'

'No,' said Arden; 'but I don't know what you mean.'

'You see,' explained the other girl, 'you find the country dreary just because you don't understand it, or recognise what's in it.'

'Yes?' queried Arden—'Well?'

'And don't you think, as you're so unhappy, it may be something the same with your life?'

'With my life?'

'With the old people up yonder, the country you're in, and all the things in the world you might do or care for——'

'I see—oh, how idle and ungrateful you think me!'

'I?—Nay, Miss Lawrance,' said Susie, making a not altogether unwelcome struggle to confess her hidden misery, lest Arden should look upon her as a preacher, a holy person; 'if I could tell you—as I can't—what sort of struggle and sin, all confused wrong and wretchedness, there is in my heart, you would know how good, and sweet, and pure, and calm, you seem to me —like a star in the dark, like a violet one doesn't look for in the lanes in January, a sort of earnest that there are better things in the world than those one just happens to have hold on — I'm not good—I can't tell you, but pray for me as an unhappy, miserable girl, who has lost the clue of right or wrong. Don't look so startled, dear Missie, I only wanted you to know how grateful I am to you for having come to see me now and again——'

'Dear Susie!' said Arden again.

'Thank you, thank you. And you will forgive me?'

'*Altro!*—I am grateful.'

'See—here's the postman!'

But there was no letter this day, either.

'You are very sorry?' said Susie.

'I—I don't quite know!'

Two or three days later she did know; two or three days later, when the desired letter came, long, kind, cordial, every phrase of it laden with allusions to the life she knew so well, the life of indolent, cultured people, familiar with all the great and beautiful places, with half the great or beautiful persons in Europe. How she longed for it again, the old, well-known, easy life! Suddenly she dropt the letter and began to cry.

'What's the matter, Sylvie, child?' asked her grandfather.

'Mrs. Rose is ill!'

'Poor thing—she's young too.'

' It's not that,' sobbed Arden ; ' it's not
dangerous, but they're going to Egypt for
the winter.'

Poor child ; she felt miserably forlorn
and forsaken ; at first nothing—not even
her picture—seemed worth desire in life.
And when her sobs calmed, and her mind
grew more at ease, the thought that chiefly
consoled her was not her yet unfinished
picture, but the memory of Susie Williams'
frank and loving face.

CHAPTER XIV.

IN THE HILL OF VENUS.

Soon after this time Arden finished her picture, and, accompanied by Mrs. Lawrance, drove into Warwick one fine afternoon and left her treasure with the frame-maker for despatch to the Birmingham Exhibition. Then there was nothing to do but to wait. The days went slowly by without event or record, while Arden wandered aimlessly about the garden, dreaming of her picture. As far as it went she knew it was good, and, though it didn't go very far, she thought it must succeed. Little did she dream how the shade of Baker would quiver with wrath over the daring greens, the uncertain breezy outlines of her work!

Now the picture was done with, it did not occur to her to visit the Farm save at rare intervals ; and, indeed, she might have soon forgotten her friends there, and the course of her story might have run in different channels, but for the aching of a tooth. So small a thing may be the hinge of Fate ! For so it was ; Arden, roaming over-late about the fields, caught a severe cold in her face, which increased till the inflamed and angry fangs tortured her by day and night to the very verge of frenzy. On the third day she came down to breakfast haggard and wild. 'Where's the nearest dentist?' was her morning greeting.

'Law, Sylvie,' cried Mrs. Lawrance, 'how scared you look, poor child! It's all that wretched tooth; it'll tarrify you and tarrify you until you've had it drarn, mark my words.'

'Why didn't you tell me sooner, then?' cried Arden. 'But I'll go at once, to-day; I can't wait. Where does he live?'

'There's a dentist at Warwick, a surgeon-dentist as they call 'un, an 'ighly respectable practioner, so they say. But you can't have the 'orse to-day, Sylvie; gran'pa's lent him to Farmer Willis.'

'How can I go, then?' cried Arden, on the brink of tears; 'and I can't bear it any longer.'

'You might waäk to Henley, Sylvie, 'tis but a matter o' four or five miles; or Raynham, that's little better nor two miles aäf, and Tuke o' Raynham's an old established man.'

'Is he a dentist, too?' cried Arden, 'oh, that's all right.'

'Not, so to speak, a surgeon-dentist, I anticipate; but 'e's drarn many a tooth in our parish. Tuke's a chemist, Sylvie.'

Arden looked up. 'I'm desperate,' she said. 'If he can't do it, I'll go to the blacksmith and have it out with a pair of tongs!'

'Law, child, how precipitate you talk!'

cried Mrs. Lawrance, 'there's no call to be so wild ; Tuke's a farmercuter, as they say; no mere Medical-hall of a man. He'll drar your tooth as well as a Birmingham operator ; not as I'm saying I'ld trust him with the stopping, leastways not gold ; still, as for tooth-drawing, a strong wrist is all that's necessary, and no man alive could make a pleasure of it——'

'Oh, don't say any more !' implored Arden ; 'I haven't the courage to stay, and soon I shan't have the courage to go.'

' 'Ere's your tea, Sylvie. Don't drink it while it's 'ot, and eat summat, child; it's exhaüstion makes you feel so vacillating and cranky.'

'Thank you.'

Mrs. Lawrance sat by for some time, looking kindly at the girl ; at last she rose and pushed back her chair.

' Well, Sylvie,' she said, ' I wish I could accompany you this morning, I'm sure ; but the bread's mixed and rising, and the

butter's ail got to be made up afore three;
then there's the dinner——'

'Oh, never mind, Mrs. Lawrance,' cried
Arden; ' I'm not afraid to go alone.'

' That's a good courage!' cried Mrs.
Lawrance, approvingly. ''E'll put you out
o' your misery in a few minutes, and I'll
mince you some nice saft mutton for your
dinner, Sylvie.'

The door closed and Arden was left alone.

To tell the honest truth, the poor child
was at no time a heroine in her endurance
of pain, and now, unnerved and prostrate,
the idea of going alone to Raynham to a
strange chemist to have her tooth drawn
presented itself to her mind as little short of
actual martyrdom. Courage!—she wanted
nothing so much as to cry on some soft
shoulder, while tender hands took care of
her and loving words consoled her. But
that was impossible. She sat still on her
horsehair chair while sympathising Betty
cleared away the breakfast, and remarked

on her melancholy looks.   Arden had half
a mind to ask Mrs. Lawrance to send
Betty with her.   But no ; she would
deserve her step - grandmother's praises :
she would show herself of a good courage.
Suddenly the agonising dart and throb
of her tooth became so violent that
Arden rushed upstairs for her cloak and
hat ; nothing could be so horrible as this.
She walked quickly through the village,
actually running when out of sight of the
houses, as nearly mad as sheer pain can
drive a poor helpless sufferer.   At last she
saw Raynham, and began to walk, but still
quickly.   The chemist's shop was at the
furthest end of the village ; the door was
standing open.

'Can I see Mr. Tuke?' asked Arden
of a little lad playing in the doorway.

The lad looked up, alert and professional at once.

'Step in, Miss, take a seat, Miss,' he
said, moving a tall chair that overtopped

his curly pate. 'Mr. Tuke, Miss, he's gone out on business; customers, he said, were to wait: he wouldn't be long.'

Arden, panting and overheated, sat down, sick at heart, in the draughty shop. No wonder that her tooth began to rage in a veritable extravagance of pain. Nothing seemed worth hoping or fearing any longer: a dull endurance took possession of her. When, at an hour's end, the thin, dapper chemist re-entered his shop, he was confronted by a pale, sunken-eyed young woman, who could only point wildly to her face, who answered all his questions with an assurance that she couldn't speak.

Fortunately Mr. Tuke soon perceived what was the matter: nothing less than acute inflammation of the jaw. He would infinitely have preferred to send so responsible a case on to the dentist at Warwick; still it was clear that not a moment must be lost. A few exclamations of genuine sympathy and concern restored sufficient

courage to Arden to enable her to sit down
in the ominous leather chair and open as
best she could her poor, swollen mouth.
Then a grating, tearing sound ; a jerk,
the tooth had broken off—then another
tug yet longer and stronger—the tooth
was triumphantly extracted, but Arden—
a senseless heap—lay crumpled on the
floor without sign or breath of life.

It was an embarrassing moment for
Mr. Tuke. In Arden's speechless condition, he had not learnt where she came from
or who she was ; and now she lay on the
floor in a salvolatile-defying swoon. He
bent over her and lifted her on to a table
in the back shop, well out of the draught,
placed a cushion under her head ; loosed
her gown, chafed her hands ; but when a
deep sigh seemed to reward his efforts, and
when at last the heavy eyelashes were
raised, it was but a moment ere the girl
sank back into unconsciousness. The poor
man was at his wits' end. An awful

suspicion came over him that she might be a sufferer from heart-complaint, that syncope might end in death. A death in his shop ; good Heavens! Mr. Tuke redoubled his efforts, and poured a glass of brandy, almost neat, down Arden's throat.

At last a faint colour struck up the whiteness of her cheeks; the little head, lost in the fallen yellow hair, began to stir uneasily upon the pillow. 'Thank God!' cried Mr. Tuke, and bent over the table to watch the return of life. And now a low moaning moved the purple lips, words followed ; Mr. Tuke stooped to listen ; he could not understand a word. She was alive, indeed, but a foreigner and delirious!

The poor fellow walked to the door and stood looking out in the street as if help might come to him thence and deliver him. The cool air fanned his forehead. He was just going to return to the inner room, when a fresh-sounding voice arrested him.

'Good day, Muster Tuke,' cried a fresh-looking man in a Whitechapel cart.

'Good day! good day, indeed!' cried the poor little chemist exasperated at this last insult of fortune. 'It's the very worst day I ever set eyes upon, that's what it is!'

'Why, what's the matter?' cried the other. 'Here; hold the horse, Teddy boy; I'm coming in.'

'I wish you would,' cried the little man, with an accent of testy relief. 'But is there anything I can do for you this morning, Mr. Williams?' he added with an instant resumption of his professional capacity.

'Let me see. Yes; there's an ounce of tartaric acid, a packet of carbonate of soda, a tooth-brush, and two penn'oth of camphor. Well! what's up this morning?'

'Just you come and see!' said Mr. Tuke in a hollow voice of mystery. He pushed open the glass-door, and there off

the table flowed a stream of golden hair,
which the dim light caught. The two men
went in together; the girl was still moaning and restlessly shifting her head from
side to side in half-unconscious, inarticu-
late pain. Her eyes were closed, her
features drawn and wan.

'Good God! It's Miss Lawrance!'
cried Harry Williams.

This was more than Tuke had dared to
hope for—all responsibility was shifted off
his hands. He began pouring the stream
of his anxiety into Harry's listening ears;
but Harry, who felt it profanation merely
to stand and worship Arden as she lay
there unconscious, could not endure the
little chemist's eager talk.

'I say, Muster Tuke,' he said at last;
'I'm sure you've had your share of
trouble. If you'll go and mind the shop,
I'll watch by Miss Lawrance.'

'Very well,' said the little man; 'there's
nothing particular to do—only when she

comes round, you just step in and call me!'

And then the glass-door shut, and Harry Williams was left alone with his unconscious companion. It was a dull autumn morning, and in the back shop, with the yellow linen blind covering the one window there was little light. It seemed a very solemn place just then, that shady parlour, with its darkened window and outstretched moaning form of a beautiful woman. Harry sat down bewildered, oppressed. Through the door he could hear Teddy pounding something in a mortar, and the sharp, querulous amazement of the chemist's voice, as he recounted his adventure to some chance customer: 'and if Farmer Williams hadn't driven home from market round by Raynham, here I should have been saddled, may be, with a nameless corpse!'

But words and sounds alike seemed strangely far away, seemed to belong to

another world than this dim, yellow-lighted
room, where the white face, unconscious in
its glory of hair, gave a solemn meaning to
its commonplace surroundings. The dull
flap of the blind against the open window,
and Arden's dreary, sighing moans were
the only sounds in the world that made a
part of this moment. At last—it seemed
after a very long while—Arden raised her
head a little, and saw, dimly outlined
against the window, the watching figure of
a man.

'Papa!' she said, in a sweet, shrill,
wandering voice.

Harry did not stir. The sweet voice
went on:

'Oh, no. Papa's dead—papa's dead
and gone. Is it Gerard that has come to
fetch me?—Gerard?'

Harry turned sharp round; suddenly,
unreasonably angry.

'No; it's me!' he said.

'A stranger!' cried Arden. 'Oh, where

am I? What's happened? What place is this?'

She sat up, leaning on her hand; her beautiful eyes wild and tired, her dress loose, her hair on her shoulders, her face still as white as death.

'Plague on me!' cried Harry Williams. 'I deserve as you shouldn't remember me, Miss Lawrance. I'm Susie's brother; and this place is Tuke's shop at Raynham, and you've been very faint, pore child—pore lady,—and I'm going to take you home.'

'Thank you,' said Arden, 'but I think I'm dying.'

Harry gave a little smile; his step-mother so often had said exactly the same thing.

'No, no,' he said caressingly as one speaks to a child; 'you're bad enough, pore child, but you're not dying. Tuke said I was to give you this.'

Arden put out a white little hand. 'You're very kind,' she said. 'I'm sorry to be such a trouble.'

'You're no trouble!' said Harry, with
an emphasis that brought a little smile to
Arden's wan face. She sat up and pushed
her hair out of her eyes. Her glance fell
upon her unfastened frock and fallen
tresses.

'The servant girl's making you some
tea,' said Harry. 'Shall she coom and
'elp you do your hair?'

'Thank you,' said Arden shyly.

'I'll send her, then.'

Harry walked out of the room into the
little front shop, where the daylight, the
orderliness of the scene, struck him as a
surprise. Was it only an hour ago he had
stopped Tuke in his doorway? He felt like
Rip van Winkle; the world seemed im-
measurably altered in that hour. Had he
known the story, he might more truly have
compared himself to Tannhäuser; for the
chemist's back parlour had been his Hill of
Venus.

CHAPTER XV.

A GOOD RESOLUTION.

An hour afterwards, Arden, wrapped from head to foot in Harry Williams' frieze overcoat, was sitting by his side in the Whitechapel cart, driving from Raynham to Arden. The chemist had made her promise not to open her mouth; so a little wan smile from time to time was all her share of the conversation. Harry spoke a little, chiefly about Susie and how ailing she had been of late; but he was thinking with a certain fierce wonder of the unknown Gerard whom Arden had called upon at waking. He had seen that she wore no ring on her left hand, and that sight had brought him a moment of acute consolation. Still there was much to be learned—much to be feared. Bah! what right had he, a mere coarse farming-man, to meddle with that beautiful angel's thoughts! He drove fast in a moody silence, until a soft little sigh from Arden caught his ears. He turned round and saw that she had gone very white.

'Don't let me faint!' she cried, putting out her hands, as if to keep off the on-coming blackness; but the life left her lips and her eyes shut. Harry put his arm round her to prevent her falling, and laid the drooping head upon his shoulder. He drove down the lane at a furious pace, the lifeless girl in his arms, and in his heart a sudden storm of passion, a fever of anxiety. They were still some little way from the village when the life came back into her face—and poor Arden, feeling very ill and wretched, began to cry like the tired child she was, the great tears rolling one after another down her face.

'Nay, nay!' cried Harry. 'You mustn't do that, Missie. We'll soon be home; only keep up your heart a little longer.'

'I—I haven't any home!' sobbed Arden.

'Pore child! Pore child! But see, that's our farm over yonder—'tis a good mile nearer than the Bushes. Stay there to-night, Miss Lawrance, dear, and Susie 'ull be so proud to take care of you.'

'No,' objected Arden; 'they'll expect me.'

'I'll go on and tell 'em,' said Harry; 'you'll be regular worn out. I declare I won't drive you any further.'

'Thank you, thank you,' sobbed Arden; 'you're really kind. I don't mean to cry, you know, only I can't help it.'

'Here we are,' said Harry, consolingly, as he turned into the clean bright farm-yard. 'Mother! Susie!'

It was very comforting to poor little

Arden to be taken possession of by friendly, gentle hands—to have all things settled with no reference to herself. In a few minutes a fire was blazing in the lavender-scented best bedroom, and she was lying wrapped in shawls, in a low chair-bedstead drawn to the hearth. A little table by her side held her cup and saucer, and a book, and by the window, Susie, as quiet as a mouse, was learning her French verbs by the fading light. Everything was home-like and easy and quiet. For some time Arden lay still, looking in the fire, and wishing she had not neglected Susie since the finishing of her picture. She was still weak and unstrung, and her own negligence and Susie's ready kindness both appeared very great affairs in her hazy conscious-ness.

'Susie!' she called at last.

Susie rose and came to the hearth, kneeling down by Arden's sofa.

'I don't think you're like the apples

and the hemlock, Susie. I think you're
the kindest person in the world.'

'Like the apples, dear?' said Susie,
fearing her friend was wandering in her
speech.

'Yes—don't you remember? You said
I only cared for you as I cared for the
orchard. And then I didn't come and see
you. But it wasn't that I didn't care—I
was so miserable.'

'And are you worrying yourself about
me?' cried Susie. 'Oh, my dear, beautiful
little Princess Sylvia, I never expected
you to care!'

'But I do,' said Arden softly, letting
one small hand rest on Susie's shoulder.

'Thank you,' said Susie reverently;
and for a long time she sat very still,
neither moving nor speaking. At last she
stirred.

'Miss Lawrance!' she said.

'Yes,' said Arden. 'I'm better.'

'Really better? Ah, yes, you look

more natural like, and your hands are warmer. Do you think you could bear to hear me tell you something?'

'Tell me something? Why, yes—of course.'

'It's not a story,' said Susie. 'It's quite true—it's dreadful. Oh, God, how can I ever have done it!'

'It's about you?' said Arden, anxiously.

'Ah, yes,' answered the other, 'more's the pity.'

She stopped for a little while and bent her head down into her knees.

'What is it, Susie dear?' said Arden. 'Please begin to tell me.'

'Yes, I must tell you, though I can't rightly judge whether I'm wrong in doing so; but when you said, dear Miss Lawrance, that you cared for me, I felt it was dishonest to hide it any longer.'

'Hide what?' queried Arden.

'Oh, me, the secret that's eating my heart out! I'm a miserable girl, and yet

I ought to be very happy, for Fred Masters loves me. But I've promised not to tell, and that's the harm of it.'

'Oh, Susie, poor little Susie!' cried Arden, sitting up on her sofa.

'I've been so miserable and so dishonest! Every time mother or Harry's done me a kindness while I've been so pettish and fractious, I've longed to ask them to strike me instead. Perhaps then I shouldn't feel so mean.'

'But why don't you tell them?' said Arden. 'It's very simple. Is your brother so *prepotente* ?'

'So what?'

'Masterful, overbearing, such a tyrant ?'

'Harry a tyrant!' cried Susie in amazement. 'Harry? Oh, he's the kindest and dearest to me of every one in the world. Why, when he was quite a lad, before I was born, he gave up his schooling to save father from the drink and all of us from ruin. If he's ever unmannerly, Miss Law-

rance, it's because he's spent his life so for
us and served us so—ever since he had
sense to see what's right and what's wrong
—that he's had no time to spend on himself. Harry a tyrant! Fancy! Why, the
first thing I remember is his teaching me to
walk ; and he used to carry me round to
all the beasts and teach me what they liked
and what we kept 'em for. But you're
looking tired.'

'No,' said Arden. 'Please go on.'

'Never was such a brother,' continued
Susie. 'All the things he'd missed he
made sure I should have—schooling, books,
leisure, time to study every day. And
when I was thirteen we lost some money in
a bank. and there was some talk of my
coming home from school at Stratford. Oh,
how I cried! And Harry wouldn't hear of
it ; he said my education shouldn't go the
same way as his, whatever happened. So
he sent me back to school, and left off
courting Rose King.'

' Oh, why did he do that ? '

' 'Cause he couldn't afford to marry.
Was'nt it fine ? '

' But what did she think, poor girl ? '

' Oh, she married Ned Swimburne. He
went a courting her the same year.'

' Did   Harry—your   brother—did   he
miss her much ? '

' I don't know.   He never said so.'

' What was she like, this Rose ? '

' Mrs. Swimburne, of Raynham ? She's
a good, comely, rosy-cheeked young woman
with four little children who all look the
same age, and a splendid dairy.'

' But how could you let him do it,
Susie ? '

' I don't know.   Harry just said he 'ld
rather I went back to school ; and I wanted
to go, ever so.'

' He's a good brother.   How could you
keep a secret from him, Susie ? '

' Ah! God only knows how hard it's
been ; and what's worse is that I know it's
wrong.'

'Why don't you tell him at once—now?'

'Now; but I promised not?'

'Still, you told me.'

'True. Oh, dear Miss Lawrance, what shall I do, I wonder?'

'Of course,' said Arden, 'you must go and tell your brother!'

'But Fred——'

'A fig for Fred! he's not fit—— I beg your pardon, Susie.'

'Oh, I know Fred's not so fine a character as Harry; but that's all the more reason why he wants me; and he loves me; and I promised him.'

'Then tell him you retract your promise.'

'Then he would think I do not trust him.'

'Because you trust your brother! What nonsense! He's much more likely to think that if you deceive your people, you'll deceive him too. Your duty's clear.

'You're sure, Miss Lawrance?'

'Quite sure.'

'I believe you're in the right,' said Susie slowly.

'Well, and when will you tell him; your brother, I mean?'

'Next Sunday, the day after to-morrow,' said Susie.

'I wish you'd tell him now,' said Arden in her petulant, tired voice. 'I can't think why you wait so long.'

'Don't you see, Miss Lawrance,' explained Susie blushing, 'I only see Fred on Sunday mornings at the school, and it would be so mean to tell without giving him fair notice. Of course I could send for him and tell him, but I never would meet him in the week for his pleasure; and just to grant him a meeting now on purpose to tell him I won't keep my promise—that would seem meaner still, don't you understand.'

'I don't understand at all!' cried

Arden; 'the mean thing is to deceive your brother!'

'Ah, yes!' sighed Susie.

'And yet,' said Arden, afraid of striking too hard, 'I'm sure you're very good, Susie, all the same!'

'It doesn't seem much like it,' said Susie sadly; 'but now you must try and sleep a little, my dear.'

Arden dozed off into a happy rest; and, sitting silently by, Susie too was not unhappy; a great peace and quietude stole into her soul. She was no longer troubled by her fault, for she had determined to renounce it, even should that renunciation include her love. She would at all hazards do the right. But as yet she was free from the penalty of doing right; as yet she still could keep the dear, strange thought that, to the man she loved, she was supremely necessary. She had not been happy before; for her conscience had left her no peace. She might not be happy hereafter, for probably she would lose her lover. But for these few blessed, quiet intermediary hours she wore, as it were, her martyr's crown and her bridal wreath together.

Her peace was strangely little troubled by Arden's obvious contempt of her lover.

She herself owned that Fred was in the wrong ; but already she was used to forgiving him. Moreover, in Susie's frank, outspoken rank of life, it was natural for unmarried girls to know what faults they might expect from their husbands. They looked for no ideals. Susie, for instance, high-principled Susie, was grieved but not surprised or shocked to know that her lover was sometimes the worse for drink. When she heard it she sighed, she did not blush. She had thought, with an admonitory heartache, that there would be so much the more pain and trouble in store for her. Susie's conception of marriage was strangely different from that of the girl who lay asleep by her side. Arden would look for

love. and care, and mutual interests. Susie
expected hard work, active management,
responsibility, labour and pain, much dis-
couragement, and possibly, in time, the
sense that her husband blamed her for being
old and faded. Yet the idea of shrinking
from such a future did not suggest itself
to her.

Some months ago Susie had done her
best to dissuade a neat little dairymaid
from marrying a drunken lout.

You know he drinks, Nan! ' she had
said.

' 'Iss, Miss.'

' And he's fond of women.'

No answer, but a curtsey.

' And he's backbone lazy.'

' 'Iss, Miss, please, Miss.   But if I har
to 'ave him, I har.'

Susie had laughed, scolded, and pitied.
It flashed across her, as she sat by Arden's
side, that her own attitude was much the
same.

CHAPTER XVI.

LOST AND FOUND.

ARDEN was delighted with the Farm.
The simple, abundant, busy life, the quaint
surroundings, the kindly, intelligent faces,
had a dignity and position of their own.
She did not feel so out of place here as in
the slovenly semi-gentility of the Bushes.
So, at least, she said to herself, prepared
to see everything rosy in a place where
she was so kindly treated. It was very
sweet to Arden to be again a person of
importance, a blessing and not a burden;
in such a sentiment, vanity and gratitude
shake hands.

She spent a happy morning, trotting
after Susie round the dairy, so clean and

fair, with its red tiles, and big yellow
bowls of creamy milk ; or round the farm-
yard, where the turkeys struck her with
dismay, and the downy yellow chickens
with delight. There were two young
calves and a litter of pigs. Arden clapped
her hands with enjoyment, and was as
pleased as a child.

Susie laughed, and petted her ; but
when Arden drew the likeness of the
youngest calf, its soft uncertain legs in
their baggy skin straddling under the
weight of the thin body and large head,
then Susie was all admiration. She did
not know how to serve enough this fair,
delicate girl, with her childish ways, her
helpless orphaned sorrow, and the gifts
and graces which appeared unmatchable
in Susie's eyes. And Arden was well
enough content to accept this lavish and
headlong admiration. For that morning,
she forgot to think of Rome.

Arden was easily persuaded to spend

that day at the Farm, and only return
to the Bushes after church with Mrs.
Lawrance on the morrow. There was
much to do at the Farm. She filled all
the flower-glasses, practised on the old
piano, chattered to Harry Williams about
the state of the crops, about Rome to
Susie, and to Mrs. Williams about her
tooth-ache.

They were all enchanted to listen ; and
by the end of dinner-time Arden considered them, save the Roses, the most
intelligent people she knew.

She had not much sense of humour,
or surely she must have laughed at the
quaint juxtaposition. The Williamses,
narrow, local, energetic, strong of mind
and strong of nature. The Roses, cultured, shallow, cosmopolitan, familiar with
a whole world of things the farmers of
West Raynham never dreamed of.

For the people of West Raynham are
of West Raynham ; they are wise in crops

and cattle; they take their politics on
Sunday from the 'Birmingham News';
and their utmost idea of strangeness or
romance is embodied in Guy Fawkes.
The people of Rome are of Rome. They
inherit three great civilisations, and claim
acquaintance alike with Trajan, Sisto
Quinto, and Victor Emanuel; they are
the next-door neighbours of Michelangelo
and Praxiteles; Nero and Seneca, the
Borgias and Savonarola, have become
familiar types to them; they have learned
the wisdom in good and evil of the Italian
Renaissance. Each set of people is, intrinsically, of equal value. The mistake
is when those from Rome, going to
West Raynham, look for Roman attributes
there.

This is what Arden did. She did not
perceive the real worth and character of
her new friends; she did not enter, as
at an opened door, into their different
mode of life, and judge it by its own con-

ditions. She did not so much as perceive that they were different. She liked them, and so she thought they resembled the other friends she also liked. She exaggerated their acquirements, and did not find out their character.

The afternoon swung by, and the two girls, who had been talking in the garden, came in to tea. Harry Williams was not in; and while Susie helped to lay the table, Arden, sitting on the settle, began to fill a quaint old punch-bowl with York and Lancaster Roses. The shadow cast by the high oaken back fell over her; she could not be seen save from the hearth.

'How late your brother is!' she said at last.

'Yes; most likely he's gone to Farmer Willis's about the harvest. He's the only man in Arden that has a proper "scarifyer."'

'A what?' cried Arden.

'A machine that rakes up the fallen

ears. I don't like it myself. I'd rather
give the poor folk their leasing.'

'Oh, dear me!' said Arden; 'what
lots of things there are I don't understand!'

'Poor little Princess! Well, I won't
trouble you any more with the Farm.
You can't be expected to take it in.
Shall I sing while you finish your roses?'

'Please, Susie, if you will.'

Susie sat down to the piano, and, with
a quaint little glance at Arden in her
shadowy nook opposite, she struck into a
fine old air—

> Who is Sylvia, who is she,
> That all our swains adore her?

The fine deep voice thrilled through
the quiet room, where the fading daylight and the flickering brightness of the
fire were contending together. The last
level sun-rays fell on Susie as she sat in
her light cotton gown, singing; her resolute head well poised; and now and then

a fitful flame lit up, among the blackness
of oak and shadows and mourning-clothes,
Arden's sweet face and golden hair, her
white swift hands moving among a lapful
of gay striped roses. Suddenly the door
was heavily flung open. Susie stopped
her singing for a second, and smiled at
her brother as he entered. But the smile
died off her face, her cheeks whitened, and
she sat still as stone, her hands upon the
keys, quite rigid and grey; while Arden,
bent over the flowers, saw nothing—was
herself unseen.

The door swung to, and Harry came
forward. He walked heavily, like an
old man, with bent shoulders and sunk
head.

'Stop your singing,' he said; and
flung himself wearily down on the red-
cushioned window-seat, huddled in his
coat, his head in his hands bent down
and hidden.

Then for a moment there was a dreadful silence in the room. It was not till some minutes after that he raised his head and spoke.

'Little maid,' he said, very gently; 'Susie!'

Susie rose. She knew what was coming.

'Come here,' he said; 'come here, Susie, and speak to thy brother.'

The girl went quietly across the room, and with a low cry she sank to the ground by her brother's side. He put his arm round her shoulder, and with the other hand he raised her face, and so for a long moment he sat, looking sadly into her hollow eyes.

'Susie, my girl,' he said at last; 'have I been a harsh brother to thee? Nay, answer me, dear; doan't cry. Why didn't you tell me, Susie, of your fine sweetheart?'

'I promised,' sobbed Susie; 'oh, dear, Harry!'

'You promised! And do words go
for such a deal, Susie, and love for
nothing? I never bad thee tell me of
thy sweethearting, that's sure enough. I
didn't think to deal with my sister like
a cozening lawyer. Susie, there should
ha' been no need of promises between us.'

'No,' said Susie. 'It was a lie, my
silence.'

'A lie!' repeated her brother. 'Think
how much it is, when we've trusted each
other so! You've been my friend as well
as my sister; and now—if you was a
man, Susie, I'd turn you from my doors;
but you poor women!'

'Oh, Harry, Harry!' sobbed the girl.
'Don't say it—don't be kind to me for
that; oh! can't I ever make it right
again?'

'No, Susie; what's done is done.
You've acted a lie! and a lie's an un-
kéd thing between friends. I can't any
longer think you the girl you was.

That's long gone by. There's an ugly
blot on your soul, Susie; and, dearly as
I love you, what can I say to the folk
who make out you've kept your body no
cleaner!'

'What?' cried the girl, starting up to
her feet; 'what, Harry?'

'Down i' th' village,' said her brother,
through his teeth, 'down there, they say
as my sister's young Masters' mistress.'

'Ah!' cried the girl, clasping her
hands across her face.

'They say cruel things,' he went on,
'a pack o' lies; but there's an ugly truth
at the bottom. They say, down there, as
you've met him at the school and at the
church, regular, for weeks past; they say,
Susie, as you made the worship of God
a cloak for your sins and shameful secrets.
And one coarse brute—I struck the lie
down his throat before he saw me—
swore, with a laugh, that he'd seen you
kiss young Masters in the church.'

'That's true,' cried Susie, coming nearer.

'And if that's true,' shouted her brother, 'by God, it may all be true! and my only sister a common woman. Keep off!'

He pushed out his arm with a movement of disgust, and but for the high settle, which stood behind her, the girl would have fallen to the ground. As it was, she leant against it, sobbing in her throat, her head drooped forward, her hands twisted.

At this moment, Arden, who had been standing horror-struck and silent by the hearth, came rapidly forward : the end of her apron was twisted through her belt, and made a loose pouch still full of roses. 'Susie!' she cried, and ran to the choking girl ; then, holding both her hands, she dragged her forwards with an impassioned movement.

'See, Mr. Williams,' she cried, ' it's Susie, Susie. Dare you doubt her ?'

' I must,' groaned Harry.

' Last night,' went on Arden, with rapid speech and flashing eyes, 'she told me all—everything ! my dear, brave, noble Susie ! She told how she had been drawn into loving a weak, vain fellow, half from compassion and half from his gay, handsome face, and how, in a weak moment, she promised for his sake to keep it a secret. And how she fretted, and was miserable at deceiving you, and how she'd always loved you since she was a baby you taught to walk.'

' Doan't 'ee,' said Harry, quickly.

' And she told me,' persisted Arden, ' that she'd been tempted often to tell you, but she dared not break her promise until she was set free. And he wouldn't release her, the coward!—(be quiet, Susie). And at last she determined to break off her engagement if needs be, and tell you herself on Sunday—to-morrow. Oh, that she had told it one day sooner !'

Harry looked up. 'Go on,' he said.

'She waited till Sunday, you know,' Arden continued, 'because—and this you mustn't be angry at—she used to see Mr. Masters at the school, and never in the week. She never would see him any day or any time you wouldn't have heard of. Never!' said Arden, bending forward with Susie's hands still clasped in hers.

'Thank Heaven for that,' said Harry; 'she's not false all through then, liar though she be.'

'How can you say so?' cried Arden; 'one false step she made, and after that her very goodness led her on and on the wrong way. She wouldn't break her promise, though she oughtn't to have made it; and then, when she determined to tell you at all risks, she wouldn't take an advantage of her lover, and waited to tell him fairly first. She's done wrong, but she's not wicked.'

'Sylvia!' cried Susie, and loosing her hands from Arden's she flung her thin, wasted arms round the neck of her friend and lay, helpless and sobbing, on that kind, protecting shoulder. For one moment her brother looked on while Arden's tender hands soothed the trembling girl. Then he got up and stood in hesitation.

'Give her me,' he said at last. 'Give me back my sister! Susie, I was wrong, deceived; you're allus my dear good girl. Speak, little maid; speak, Susie!'

He took her gently in his arms. She lifted up her face, streaming with tears. 'But I love him, Harry,' she cried; 'don't think I consent to hate him! If he came into the house now I should know it. I should know if he was out in the lane. I should go to him and forgive him. You mustn't forgive me, Harry, until you know. I love——'

The words failed from her lips, and

her head fell back. Great sobs choked her utterance.

'Pore ! child,' said Harry. 'I know ; I know. Don't take on so, darling. My poor little sister, the worst is done with now !'

CHAPTER XVII.

FRIENDS.

POOR Susie lay, speechless and senseless, on her bed upstairs, with her mother watching beside her. She had now been ill for thirteen days with a low nervous fever, not dangerous but slow. It was perhaps the kindest thing that Fate could have sent her, releasing her from thought, and triply endearing her to the hearts of those she had wronged and wounded; so that now she lay quiet in a lethargy of weakness, while her future was decided for her. Downstairs, Arden, who had been persuaded to stay on and help Mrs. Williams in watching Susie, was talking to Harry. They were sitting on either side

the hearth, deep in conversation, the broad-
shouldered farmer in his shiny broadcloth,
and the delicate, refined young girl :
despite all difference, they talked like old
friends, for favouring circumstances had
brought them close together.

'I think she's better to-day, Mr.
Williams,' Arden was saying, as she
stooped towards the fire to see the colours
of her crewel-work. She chose the proper
strand, and threaded her needle. 'I shall
have to go home again soon,' she went on.

Harry shuffled uneasily on his seat.

'It 'ull be hard work to spare you,
Miss Lawrance.'

'Now that's very sweet,' said Arden :
'I'm sure at the Bushes they did not find
it hard work at all. They were only too
pleased!'

'I can't think it likely,' said Harry
Williams.

'*Altro*!' cried Arden. 'But I can't
bear them any grudge, for I have been as

happy to stay as they were to spare me.
I've been very happy here.'

'You're very good, I think,' said her
companion. 'You've come into our house
in our sore need, and made us happy in
spite of it, and taken a share all the same
as if you was one of us. If that's your
happiness, Miss Lawrance, 'tis a blessed
gift.' He spoke so seriously that the easy
tears rose to Arden's eyes.

'Ah!' she cried, clasping her hands in
her pretty foreign way, 'that's what I was
dying for—to belong to some one, and take
a share. In my grandfather's house I
never was at home.'

Harry went very red. It seemed impossible that she could mean that she belonged to them, mere farmer people ; that
she found this house of his a home. He
tried to look as though he had not heard,
while the words sang and rang in his ears
like a peal of wedding bells.

'And here, you see,' went on Arden,

'there really seemed a place for me. Oh, I never could forget that first morning when your mother, half distracted, kept asking poor, unconscious Susie where she had put the key of the linen-cupboard. Why is it that the saddest things make one laugh as much as one cries?'

'Do they?' said Harry, grimly. 'They make me wish to knock that villain down again, and harder nor the first time, too.'

'Do you know where he's gone?' Arden inquired.

'Not I, nor care, neither. He's a bad 'un wherever he may be; but I've done with him since he's gainsaid that wicked gossip as far as in him lay, and I did give him a good 'un in the eye,' Harry chuckled.

'I think you were quite excusable,' cried Arden. 'I don't blame you at all, for my part.'

'Blame me, Miss Lawrance? Why, I

couldn't ha' done less for my sister. I
couldn't ha' done less.'

It seemed so comic to Arden, this favour
of knocking out for one the teeth of one's
lover, that she began to laugh, to the evi-
dent offence of her hearer. Country people
are shy of being laughed at, and Harry
was no exception to the rule. But after a
moment he seemed to forgive her, regarding
the pretty little figure with a pitying smile.

'You're so young,' he said; 'it comes
handiest to you to laugh at all th' events
of life. But 'tis pore work, pore work,
laughing at men's villainies. And for the
matter of that 'tis poor work enough
wreaking one's anger on the scoundrel.
Easy enough to knock him down and turn
him out o' his parish; but, none the less,
my dear little sister (so merry, so clever
with her fingers as she used to be) is lying
upstairs like a senseless log.'

Harry dropped his head between his
hands, and stared gloomily into the fire.

'Hadn't it been for you, Miss Lawrance,' he went on, 'I think I should ha' been tempted to curse God ; so awful was the blow. Fancy, in one hour to have all I most believed in changed to a deceit, a wicked cheat! I was a'most too dumbfoundered to be angry, even. Oh, I thought Susie 'ld ha' told me 'twas all a lie; but when she stood there, and let me say what I would and think what I would, without so much as a shake o' th' 'ead, I —I—oh, 'twas too much for me !'

' Don't think of it !' said Arden softly. She had left her seat, and was kneeling in front of the fire, warming her hands.

' Nay,' said Harry, looking down at the sweet face lit by the fire-flicker, 'nay, I'll rather think how, in the worst and thick of the trouble, you came forward, with them striped roses in your apron falling on the floor one by one. And your words was sweeter than any roses, red or white, for they gave me back my trust in little Susie;

nor any blessèd angel out of heaven cudn't seem more marvellous-like to a man, or more full of pity and kind mercy, than you did then, Miss Lawrance, holding the little un' up in your arms till I cud take her back with a willing heart.'

Arden put out her hand. 'Thank you,' she said.

'''Tis you, Missie, I must thank. I thought I'ld like you to know, that's all. But you're crying, I declare!' exclaimed Harry in dismay. 'What can I ha' done? What can I ha' said? Great orkerd brute I am.'

'Nothing,' said Arden; 'I'm quite happy. Only, you see, I'm—I'm not used to having any friends.' Harry stared. 'At least,' she went on, 'I've got three friends in Italy, only I don't know where they are. But that's so far away! I've got no friends here,' she said in a piercing tone.

'Oh, Missie!' said Harry Williams.

'Except you all,' went on Arden, 'all of you. Don't you see that's what I'm crying for?'

'Oh!' said Harry, blankly.

'Because,' explained Arden, 'I'm so glad. Because we are friends now, aren't we?'

'Miss Lawrance,' said the poor, bewildered farmer, 'if you'll have us for friends, as love and honour and thank you, and will do all our lives; if you'll take us for your humble friends, 'tis but like your sweetness and goodness. I can't say more.'

'Ah,' said Arden very softly, 'it's all settled then! We're friends now.'

They sat a little longer alone in the brown, dim parlour; but neither cared to say anything more after that. At last Arden went upstairs into the room where Susie was lying, so still and quiet. She sent Mrs. Williams downstairs and set herself by the white, peaceful bed. There was no sound, save now and then the yelp of the watch-dog, or the sleepy chirp of a half-awakened bird. Arden was happy. She was thinking how nice it was to be good, to be of some use in the world, and how natural it came to her when she was not crossed. This was the sort of life she had meant to lead when she left Italy behind; it was a sweet, noble life, she thought. She could not help feeling that she made a very picturesque figure in that troubled household; but her vanity was so innocent and artless that it only brought out the sweetest lines in her face—a wistful, yearning, devoted look. Just then Susie woke and turned round.

'Sylvia!' she whispered.

Arden bent over her and kissed her softly.

'Dear Sylvia,' said the weak, tired voice. 'I'm at peace now, at peace. You've saved me, Sylvia!'

CHAPTER XVIII.

THE LITTLE RIFT.

' WELL, my dear Mrs. Masters, I am sure you will never repent of your generous decision.'

The Rector was standing in Mrs. Masters' drawing-room, rubbing his long white hands and smiling, as he prepared to take his leave.

' Don't go, Mr. Law,' said his hostess; ' or I shall think you came for nothing else but to wring a promise out of me! '

The Rector drew up a chair and sat down.

' It is seldom difficult to persuade you to generosity,' he said.

' I don't know about that,' answered

Mrs. Masters, drawing back her long neck with a quick, habitual bridle. 'I don't think I like being persuaded. But certainly I hate to do anything mean.'

'It will be a kind and delicate attention to go and see the poor girl. She has really behaved very well,' said Mr. Law, with an appeal in his voice.

'And Fred behaved very badly, you mean, I suppose? Poor Fred!' Mrs. Masters gave an impatient sigh. 'Well, I acknowledge she has turned out more reasonable than I expected.'

'I applaud her determination, for my part,' affirmed Mr. Law; 'unequal marriages are seldom fortunate.'

'He was regularly trapped into the engagement, I consider, poor boy!' cried Mrs. Masters. 'It was a most preposterous notion; but I won't quarrel with the girl, since she has given him up.'

'It must have been an effort to resign him,' said the sagacious Rector.

'It was, no doubt. Indeed, I should have gone to see her before—it was my natural impulse—but for the absurd scene that brother of hers made with my poor boy. I believe he considers it all his doing that I have sent Fred away for a while—out of his yellow-haired sister's clutches.'

'Well, well,' said the Rector, in his most deprecating voice ; 'we are agreed that she has relaxed them.'

'Yes ; and I have agreed to be magnanimous. But I shall expect a great deal of applause, I forewarn you.'

'You never cease to deserve it, my dear friend,' declared the Rector. 'But now I must go and see old Mrs. Barnes. I promised to be there by four.'

Mr. Law rose and took his leave, well pleased with his success ; for he knew the most effectual answer to all village slanders would be for Fred's mother to call upon Susie. Now she had given her promise he knew she would not fail. But Mrs.

Masters chafed sorely against the bonds
she had forged for herself, and from which
there was no honourable escape. For a
long time she wandered up and down her
drawing-room like a wild creature in a
cage. Oh, the hateful promise! It was
too much to expect of her. She took up a
book and threw it down again; began her
work only to throw it aside. At last she
rang the bell.

'Don't get the tea till five,' she ordered;
'I am going into the village.'

Thus it happened that on the last day
of Arden's stay at the farm a loud knock
was heard at the entrance door. Susie was
lying on the sofa, still pale and weak;
Arden had picked up the 'Siege of Dinant,'
and was kneeling by the fire to catch the
light on her page, while Farmer Williams,
who had just come in from his turnip-fields,
delivered a solemn warning, with inflammation of the eyes at the beginning and
total blindness at the end of it. Arden

laughed. Then came the knock at the door.

'Who can be there?' cried Susie. 'The carrier's gone by hours ago.'

'P'r'aps Mr. Law's stepped round,' suggested her brother.

'Oh, no, he came yesterday. I wonder if Betsy heard the bell. Yes. Why it's somebody coming in,' said Susie.

Arden dropped her book and rose to her feet; her cheeks, burned red by the fire, blushed to a deeper colour when she perceived the tall, handsome woman who entered the room.

'Mrs. Masters!' cried Susie, going very white.

'Yes, my dear,' said the great lady. 'Now pray don't excite yourself; lie still : I'm sure you are still very delicate.'

Susie couldn't answer, so many memories choked her throat.

Mrs. Masters went on, giving her time to recover : 'What a charming home you have here—really most picturesque, I de-clare! It would be quite a *trouvaille* to an artist, I assure you, quite a treasure-trove! It has been in your family a great many years, I think, Mr. Williams?'

'Two centuries and more,' growled Harry.

'Yes. No wonder you are proud of it. And how is your mother, Miss Williams?'

'I will go and tell your mother, Susie,' said Arden, glad of an excuse to escape. As she closed the door behind her she heard Mrs. Masters say—

'A relation of yours, I suppose.'

Somehow she felt very angry. She called Mrs. Williams, and then went up-stairs to her own room.

A relation of the Williamses! Was that another insult of Mrs. Masters'? Arden looked in the glass. The neat foreign dress, the graceful figure, the re-fined face, were reassuring to see. She wondered what pleasure Mrs. Masters

could find in persecuting her. Of course,
she did not look like a relation of the
Williamses. She began to smile a little
bitterly as she contrasted her own image
with Susie's Raynham frocks, and Mrs.
Williams in her wonderful caps. 'Perhaps,' Arden thought, 'I have been wrong
in letting myself drift into an intimacy
with such people.'

The bare thought startled back her
customary frame of mind. How silly she
was to care what Mrs. Masters chose to
fancy! The Williamses were her good
friends, and she should know whom she
liked. She would give Mrs. Masters no
occasion for patronising her; that, at least,
was certain. At this moment she heard
Mrs. Williams calling her in the passage.
'I'm coming, dear Mrs. Williams!' cried
Arden, and flew to the door. She had
never noticed before how much like an
upper servant the little woman looked.

'Is Mrs. Masters gone?' inquired
Arden.

' Yes, Miss Lawrance,' said her hostess.
' And tea's ready if you'll come, Miss
Lawrance.'

Arden ran down the staircase and flung
herself on her knees by Susie's sofa.

' Oh, I'm so glad that woman is gone!'
she cried. ' Hasn't she tired you to death,
poverina, with her awful voice and her condescending manners ; " *Non ragioniam' di
lor, ma guarda e passa.*" '

Arden sprang to her feet and struck an
attitude. ' Really quite a *trouvaille*!' she
exclaimed. ' Most picturesque, I'm sure.'

Though the farmer roared with delight
at Arden's mimicry, Susie would not laugh.
' Now, that's ill-natured of you, Sylvie,' she
cried. ' It was really kind of her to come
and see me.'

' Maybe 'twas kind and maybe 'twas
impertinent,' growled her brother. ' Leastways, I'm one with Miss Lawrance ; I
doan't like her.'

' Nor do I,' cried Arden. ' But she

thought Harry's speech had never sounded so broad before.

All tea-time, the quartette—usually so peaceable—seemed to be playing a game of cross-purposes ; for Mrs. Williams, who thought the visit an immense honour and satisfaction, kept appealing for sympathy which Arden would not give.

' She's an odious woman ! ' she declared at last.

' La ! Miss Lawrance, how you take my breath away ! ' cried little Mrs. Williams. ' Why, Mrs. Masters is a born Arden.'

' One would think you lived here under the feudal system ! ' cried the indignant girl.

' Well, Princess Sylvia,' said Susie, ' one may say there's never been a time when there hasn't been an Arden at the Hall and a Williams at the Farm. 'Tis natural we should feel our position.'

' *Mi da sui nervi !* ' cried Arden, and jumping up from the table she went to the hearth and picked up her book. But she did not read; she felt that she had behaved ungraciously, and that is not a pleasant feeling for a saint and a heroine. At last she looked up and saw the farmer standing by her, looking at her with grave concern.

'I've been very rude,' cried Arden, with a charming gesture; 'will you excuse it for this once?'

'La! Miss Lawrance,' said Harry, 'there's nothing to overlook. Of course you're not used to know coarse, orkerd folk like us.'

Arden was immediately propitiated.

'Oh, yes, I am!' she cried, running to kiss Susie. 'You're my real friends, my only friends in England.'

She behaved so sweetly during the **rest** of the evening that no one guessed—not even she herself—of the little rift within the lute. It was her last night at the Farm.

The next morning she went to her

grandfather's house. The two old people did their best to welcome her; Mr. Lawrance tired himself with asking questions and telling old jokes, and Mrs. Lawrance got out her best quince marmalade for tea. But Arden missed the real gladness that her presence had called out at the Farm; she had, in fact, been made so much of there that the pathos and friendliness of this meagre little welcome home seemed quite flat and insignificant.

She sat quietly in her place at table.

'You're looking but poorly, child,' began Mrs. Lawrance, after a long and silent inspection. 'You're no credit to the Farm with them pale cheeks.'

'We'll freshen 'em up a bit, Nannie,' said the old gentleman. 'She's missed her drives, I'll warrant; they've got no pony carriage at Williams's.'

'Oh, they have,' cried Arden, 'a spring-cart, grandpapa, and such a nice fat old horse! I used to drive to Raynham nearly

every day to fetch Susie's medicine from
the chemist's.'

'Pore child,' said Mrs. Lawrance in her
most commiserating drawl. 'I've never
rightly forgiven myself that I let yer go to
Tuke's alone.'

'Never mind,' said Arden. 'If you had
taken me, I should never have gone to stay
at the Farm.'

'Well, well,' old Mr. Lawrance began,
'I shall have to go and ask Mrs. Williams
what weed they squirted on your eyes to
make you so enchanted.'

'They were very glad to see me,' said
Arden, simply; but the sentence had an
unfortunate ring, and alas! Mrs. Lawrance
was never wise in time.

'You can't say, Sylvie,' she began, in
her plaintivest voice, 'as your grandpa's
not been glad to see you, and I too, when
you're amiable. But sometimes you are
that fratchetty and discontented-like, I
haven't it on my conscience to look

pleased. But if you consider, as you appear to intimate, as we grudge you the bit of food——'

'I'm sure——' began Arden indignantly.

'Nay, nay, she didn't mean it, Nan; she said nought that was capable of giving offence,' put in the old gentleman. 'You're a good little girl, Sylvie, and we're both glad to see you about again, child.'

'Thank you, grandpa.'

'Just fetch me the big Shakespeare, there's a good girl. 'We're reading Hamlet in the evenings now.'

Arden fetched the book, and for an hour her grandfather's slow and husky voice was the only sound in the room, dim-lighted with the one candle, placed between her grandfather's book and Mrs. Lawrance's work-basket.

At last the act was finished, and 'the book put away.

'I've been thinking, dear,' said Mrs. Lawrance, stooping over her husband, 'as we 'aven't shown Sylvie that parcel the carrier braüt her yesterday.'

'All right, all right!' said the old gentleman; 'she can wait till the morning, I suppose!'

But Mrs. Lawrance had already opened the cupboard door, where Arden spied a high, narrow wooden case. It was her picture sent back from Birmingham.

CHAPTER XIX.

PIGSKIN WILL LAST.

MR. LAWRANCE, quoting his favourite author, had often told his grandchild how misfortunes come, not as single spies, but in battalions ; yet Arden, notwithstanding the rejection of her picture, was quite unprepared to defer still longer the hope of meeting her childish friends again. Her thoughts often turned to Gerard and Ellie, for she was not of a nature to forget, and the few impressions that her nature ever really received were very lasting. She had, therefore, been grieved when the Roses had left her so long without writing, and when, about a week after her return home, the postman brought her a letter from Cairo, she could hardly open it for the very nervousness of her eager pleasure.

At last she made up her mind to read the letter, and breaking open the envelope discovered the precious thin sheets ; not quite as precious as they might have been, for they were written in Ellie's hand, but still a memorable feast for that hungry and fasting little heart.

She began to read—

'Shepherd's Hotel, Cairo.

'Dear Arden,—Yesterday's mail brought a whole sheaf of your letters, which had been lying at our Roman apartment until we could forward a reliable address. Gerard says you will think us very heartless ; and mother asks me to send you a line at once, as she doesn't begin to get any stronger yet. I can't say I feel much like writing letters, for there is absolutely nothing to say. It is much pleasanter reading yours. I fear you are not having a good time at

your grandfather's place. It must be a
"one-horse consarn," as Daniel Willis used
to say. I should think even Daniel Willis
would be an enlivenment. Where do you
shop? You cannot get your clothes at
Warwick, I presume. They will send over
from the Bon Marché in the Rue du Bac;
but it is always a risk trusting to measure-
ment. You may, however, be quite certain
of their gloves; they are excellent. It is
very different shopping here; the stores
are very dear, and I cannot say I ever feel
certain that their style is quite the latest
thing. One has a feeling that it was very
novel yesterday. I don't believe but you
might get something at Leamington. The
Sargents once spent a winter there. They
found it very dull; no theatre : all the
people hunt, for an excitement. They went
back to Boston the week before we left
Rome. Mollie sent you her affectionate
regards; she is grown very intellectual,
and has let her bang grow long. Well, I

can guess it is in anticipation of Boston. All this time I have not told you how we are. Mother coughs more than she used to do, I am afraid; but her spirits never run down; mine do, I must declare: one feels so outlandish here, and I don't believe I like having no *femme de chambre*. All the servants in the hotel are men and natives. Gerard says I am very parochial. We left Elise at Marseilles with her relations. Perhaps that is why I feel so dull. One can't have a good time with all the responsibilities of one's wardrobe hanging over one. It is awful to think how we shall get those trunks across the desert; we shall never do it in the world! Gerard is looking very well. He is quite devoted to sketching. The other day he met Miss De la Rue in a mosque; he is devoted to her also. Do you remember how he used to rave about her? But that was at Newport, before your time. Anyhow she used to snap her fingers at his ravings.

She has quite lost her looks, and is dying
of consumption. I must say if I had to
die I should like the complaint to be-
coming, or else I should not be on view to
my admirers. We are going on to Syria
after Christmas, to Mount Lebanon, Mount
Hermon, the Mount of Olives, the Holy
Land, the "entire figure," to quote Dan
Willis again. I shall feel like crying for joy
when I can look forward to going no further
than down Beacon Street. I don't think I
should love to live in Europe for a finality;
but I suppose this is not Europe. Here
we appear to be always on the go. If we
survive the desert and the brigands, we
shall be in Rome in May ; then we are to
stay a month with the Curtises at Pegli.
I presume we shall go home *viâ* Leghorn ;
we would all prefer starting from Liver-
pool; but it depends on mother's health.
If she is sick, she will go as much as
possible by sea. I must say I shall think
it hard if we do not spend a week or so in

Paris. Gerard said I was to tell you that
if we stop in London, he shall run down
to Arden and fetch you up to spend a day
with us at our hotel. Does one say "down"
or "up" to London ? I know there is a
superstition. Gerard would have put in a
line but he is dining with the De la Rues.
He is quite in the swim, and knows all the
best people. I have to stay at home with
mother. Gracious! what a long letter I
have written ; it is so difficult to stop
when one has fairly got started off. I
suppose I may as well stop here as anywhere else. Mother sends her kindest
love, and I remain, dear Arden,

  ' Your ever affectionate friend,

     ' ELLIE.

 · P.S.—I forgot to tell you we shall be
at this address until New Year. After
then our letters should be sent care of the
U.S. Consul, Beyrout, Syria.'

Arden crunched the letter in her hand

with a certain feeling of indignation. Her
long, frequent, tender letters, 'a whole sheaf
of them,' had deserved something more than
this frivolous reply. Perhaps she should
have found some satisfaction in the well-
meant and friendly little letter; but the starv-
ing beggar to whom you give a stone does
not use it to stop a chink in his hovel wall :
he is more likely to hurl it at your head.
And Arden, usually so gentle and girlish,
felt for a moment a passion of anger when
she finished Ellie's epistle—the Rue du
Bac, Mollie Sargent's fringe, Beacon Street !
were these fit answers to her expressions
of affection, her appeal for sympathy? So
she asked her burning spirit, revolted at
Ellie's lukewarmness. But she never repeated to herself that phrase concerning
the fair Miss De la Rue ; and yet this
disaffection of Gerard's was perhaps the
wounding point of the letter. Not that
she had ever so much as fancied herself in
love with him. But Gerard was her oldest

friend, her special chum; she relied on him
to remember her. And already it seemed
he was so engrossed with newer friends
that he could not spare the moment to
send her a line of good wishes. And then
the phrase floated up to her lips about the
Roses' having known Miss De la Rue at
Newport 'before your time.' Her time!
It had begun when she was eight years old,
nearly ten years ago. And now they could
put off her desperate need, her hopes, her
clinging affection, with stupid phrases
about Daniel Willis and the difficulties of
provincial shopping! But all the while
that her lips blamed Ellie, her heart was
sore with Gerard.

She seized her hat and rushed out of
the house, with the letter still crumpled in
her hand. She began walking quietly, as
was her habit when greatly moved, up the
orchard path into the hill meadow; there
she sat down on the burnt grass on the
brow of the rise, and, throwing off her hat,

let the cool morning wind blow in her hair. The breeze, the large, simple view, the loneliness, enveloped her with a certain quiet. But she felt very sad, very deserted and desolate. She fell to thinking of old times, of her happy Roman childhood—oh, what would she not give to find the mere outside of it again! to hear the noise of the fountains in the streets, to see the endless steps of the Trinità dei Monti, with the branches of flowering trees, from the gardens behind, waving over the low brown walls, to hear the sweet voices of the nuns floating down it! She remembered the little ring her father had given her—it was on her finger to-day : the same, only a little worn and small ; as the love of Rome was in her heart. Her father had wished to leave Rome, the Roses had forgotten her easily enough. Was she the only person who cared to be constant? In her present frame of mind the fancy galled her. Henceforth she would care no more for her friends than they cared for her. And then there drifted out of the forgotten places of her memory Ellie's childish phrase about making friends of people passing through. Let them do it! Ah, she thought, they had always done it! She was, and had been, no more to them than Daniel Willis, Mollie Sargent, any chance amusing new-comer; and she had given them her very heart in exchange. She felt tricked, insulted, sore. She would no longer care for them; she would answer Ellie on her own terms.

' Miss Lawrance!' said a friendly voice from the gate.

She looked up; there stood Harry Williams, leaning over the rail and looking anxiously towards her. He seemed a sort of screen between her and the dreadful, wearying memory of the past. She jumped up and ran down the hill to the gate, and stood there; one hand with the letter in it held to her side, and the other reached out in friendly greeting.

'Oh, I am so glad to see you!' she cried. 'Come in and talk to me; I feel so lonely.'

She held the gate open with an inviting smile, and of course the hapless farmer entered.

It was indeed a wonderful moment for him. He had missed Arden sorely; his home had seemed but a sunless place without that glancing presence. All the force of a dogged and obstinate nature he had centred on her as its prize, all the passionate devotion of his heart. He had never seen any one like her. She was so good, so beautiful, so sweet and friendless. And yet—even while he longed to protect and champion her—to shower all manner of love and service upon her—he never lost sight of the barrier between them, the barrier of rank and position which, from his standpoint, it appeared impossible to over-

leap. His father had married above him
indeed, but not a lady like Arden, who was
the loveliest lady he had ever seen. He
had expected when he saw her again that
she would have drifted further apart from
him, now that she was out of his house and
had returned to the company of her own
people. But instead she had flown to him
like a bird to its nest—had run to him with
open arms. Poor Harry, ignorant of the
truth and putting the most favourable con-
struction on Arden's welcome, was wandering in a Fool's Paradise of delight. Although he loved her so dearly, he felt an
acute thrill of joy when he realised
her lonely and friendless life. She might
come to him so for warmth and shelter:
would not he gladly spend the dearest forces
of his heart in her defence and service?

All this while these two persons, thinking so differently, were strolling side by
side up the steep rise of the meadow.
Arden, who was weary of her thoughts,

so much less sweet than her companion's, broke the silence.

'This isn't like *your* pastures, Mr. Williams,' she began, smiling in his face and thrusting the little point of her shoe into one of the great fissures in the turf.

'''Tain't in very good condition,' assented Harry, too much engrossed with the smile and the foot to care very much about the land.

'What should you do with it if it were yours?' inquired Arden.

'If t'wur mine?' said Harry, with a look of bewildered, impossible gladness. 'Oh, the land you mean?'

'Of course,' said Arden. 'What should you do?'

'Well, you see, Miss Lawrance, this land's in reg'lar bad condition. I should turn it up and drain it and drench it with good manure—them Brummagem oyster-shells 'ud do, button-waste and stuff—and

so I should let it lay fallow for a season ;
potatoes then 'ud be the most likely thing,
and the next year t'wud be fit for cereals
and roots, or you cud lay it down in grass
for the dairy.'

'I wish it *were* yours!' cried Arden :
'it's a pity to see everything falling into
rack and ruin for want of a little
care.'

'And so you wish t'wur mine,' said
Harry, more than ever charmed. 'I wonder
what th' attorneys 'ud make of you, Miss
Lawrance ?'

'I'm afraid no one would make much
of me,' cried Arden. 'I'm a failure !'

Harry began to laugh ; but, seeing that
she really looked sad and almost bitter, he
stopped and gazed at her anxiously.

'D'ye think so ?' he said very gently.
'You mustn't give way like that, Missie :
'tis only that you're moped and moithered
up at the Bushes, with the old gentleman
so ill, and Mrs. Lawrance——'

He stopped short.

Arden began to laugh. 'Oh, it isn't only that!' she cried, and then Harry saw the letter crumpled in her hand.

'Bad news!' he said. 'Pore child, I'm sorry.'

'Yes,' replied Arden, touched by his concern, 'it is bad news, although no one's dead, or ill, or anything of that sort.' She glanced up at him. He looked so kind that she went on; 'but, you see, these are my very oldest friends—my very oldest—and they seem to have forgotten all about me already. It's very soon!' said Arden, with tears in her voice.

'Brutes!' ejaculated Harry, clenching his fist.

'No,' said Arden, 'they're awfully nice so long as you're there. Every one—and they most of all—used to be so sweet to me. And now not one—not one—remembers me.'

Harry did not speak at first, but as she waited he burst out :

' I'ld like to punish 'em, I would ! '

Arden smiled. She had felt so weak and desolate that this ferocious championship was welcome to her.

' We won't punish them,' she said, with a wan smile, ' we'll forget them ! '

' T'aint so easy forgetting,' said Harry, carried out of himself by her appeal to his sympathy. ' Haven't I tried by day and night to forget thy sweet little face by my hearth and thy clear voice in my ears ?— And all no use, no use.'

Arden looked up frightened. ' Mr. Williams ! ' she cried.

' Yes—me—Williams,' he went on, with a moment of passionate self-assertion; ' look down on me as much as you like. No doubt you'll niver speak to me again. But love is stronger than many waters as I've read in the Bible, and though I know I'm a fool—an uplifted, foolish dreamer—I've dared to love you, dear. How cud I help it ? '

Arden said nothing.

' How cud I keep thinking,' he went on, ' as you're a lady born and I a rough orkerd lout of a farmer, when I found you lying senseless in Tuke's little parlour ; and when I took you home, so childish and frightened-like as you wur ; and then when you came out like an angel and gave me Susie back ? How cud I help it, Miss Lawrance, think of that.'

' Yes,' said Arden timidly.

' Not as ever I hoped, in my sober senses, as I cud be more to you than Susie's brother. But, for all that, the thought of you is allus with me. I get no peace by day and night. Oh, God, how hard it is that I should be so different ! '

' Don't,' said Arden, laying a light little hand on his arm, for his passion was piteous to witness.

' It must be so ! ' said the farmer more

calmly. 'I must just look on, I suppose, while they slight you and moither you to death. But if ever you want summat as I can do, Missie, you'll remember I'm allus there.'

'Thank you,' said Arden.

'And you woan't be hard on Susie? Poor child, 'tis not her fault, and she fair worships you, Miss Lawrance. I'll keep out of your sight. I'll not trouble you any more, I promise. But you woan't remember it agen the little 'un?'

'No,' said Arden.

'I'll leave you now then, Miss Lawrance. Forgive me if I've taken a liberty as frightens you. 'Twoan't happen agen. Good-bye.'

'Oh, I'm so sorry!' cried Arden.

'Nay, doan't 'ee be sorry; my life's the sweeter to me, as well as bitterer. I'll be a better man for't henceforrard. I'll keep the memory of your sweet goodness in my heart, and I woan't be so hard to them as have wronged me. But now I'll leave you, Missie. Good-bye.'

He turned slowly round, without reaching out his hand.

'Stay,' cried Arden. 'I don't think I want you to leave me!'

CHAPTER XX.

I'LL LOVE YOU TRUE.

An hour afterwards Arden was upstairs,
safe in her room at the Bushes. As yet
she did not realise the promise she had
made ; she did not understand all that she
had implied when she had told her lover
that he might stay—that she would accept
his love and service. She had not promised
to love him. She had told him to wait
and hope. She felt frightened now ; she
would willingly draw back. And yet she
was proud that so strong a heart should
own her sway. To do her justice Arden
did not think, in that moment, of the
difference of rank between her lover and
herself. In that hour of fear and hope,

and bashful new-born passion, she merely
was a woman and he a man; she the
defenceless, he the would-be lord and
servant and protector. She feared, not to
condescend, but to surrender.

This mood passed, and Arden grew aware
that her lover was a squire of low degree:
that he did not look or speak or think the
same as, for instance, Gerard Rose. But
in her present soreness of heart the difference was welcome. Let go the conven-
tional polish and the shallow smoothness,
cried her spirit; choose the substantial
worth plain and solid. She wanted a
refuge from herself, and from the world,
and Harry was strong and kind and sure.
Nor did Arden realise to the full how
much lower than hers was his social and
intellectual platform. She had lived so
little in England, knew absolutely nothing
of English society. The English she had
known were birds of passage, all alike in
the boarding-house equality of Brown and

Brabazon. They were all foreign names to her, Williams as good as Arden; and the language too was foreign. She did not think the ' dialect,' as she called it, a stamp of commonness ; the difference between the tongue of an Albizzi of Florence and a Borghese of Rome, between the people of Milan and the people of Naples, was as marked as the difference between the speech of Harry Williams and of Gerard Rose. Of course he was only a farmer. But Arden's imagination was impressed by the picturesque roominess of the old Farm in which his family had lived for more than two hundred years in homely plenty and comfort. Among the Americans she had known, travelled and cultured *nouveaux riches*, among the painters and singers living here and there, wherever a studio was good and cheap, such a thing was impossible. She found the idea full of dignity, of repose. She would be glad of such a resting-place.

She sat quiet, trying to think, and ever finding her thoughts float off into a dream, until the little servant came to call her to dinner. And when she went down she said nothing about the things which had happened that morning. They seemed, indeed, unreal. But as she sat quiet afterwards, in the dusk, she heard a sudden ring at the bell and Harry's voice in the hall. So it was to be all made known, it was neither a secret nor a dream! She started up to make her escape, but the door opened and Harry took her hand.

'I want you to stay and listen, Sylvie,' he said.

Mr. Lawrance, asleep in the great old velvet chair, started out of his doze and looked round him.

'What, Williams?' he began, 'so you've come to see my little girl. Very kind of you, I'm sure, very kind! She never stops telling us of all the charms and wonders of the Farm.'

Mr. Lawrance was quite awake now. He looked, Arden thought, more dignified and impressive than she had ever seen him : there appeared a difference she never had noticed before between the old gentleman, urbane and condescending, in his rumpled old clothes, and the high-coloured black-haired farmer in his glossy broadcloth and blue tie, awkwardly smiling through a blush, as he twisted the brim of his hat in his hands. She wished it were over, settled, either way.

'Mr. Williams has come to see you, grandpapa, not me,' she said.

'Eh?' cried the old gentleman, 'come to see me, has he? Anything wrong with the fences again, Mr. Williams?'

'No, Mr. Lawrance. Not as I know of,' said Harry sheepishly. 'I've made bold to mend them rails in the Five Acre. But it's not of such every-day business as I be come to speak.'

Arden blushed. 'I think I'll go,' she said.

'Nay, Sylvie, wait a bit,' cried her lover. 'Mr. Lawrance, doan't you see what's up? I've come to ask you if I may see Miss Sylvie to pay her my addresses-like. I know it is a bold thing for the likes of me to love her; but I do!'

'Dear me!' cried Mr. Lawrance, settling his spectacles to look the better at the young farmer, 'this is very unexpected—very. I really can't commit myself to an opinion.'

'No wonder,' said Harry, 'as you should think me uplifted. So I be; so I be. But I doan't want Missie here to pledge herself to anything. 'Tis only a chance to make her bear with me as I ask for. She's free as air, Mr. Lawrance; and if she doan't grow fond of me by-and-by there's no occasion as she should go any further. 'Tis a wife I want, not a slave.'

Arden looked up. She liked to see him so, bold and modest.

'Well, well, Sylvie,' said her grandfather, 'I suppose you must go your own
gait ; I can't interfere. But I can't imagine you a farmer's wife, child.'

'There's no call, Mr. Lawrance, as
you should fancy her any different. I cud
keep my wife like a lady, I'm proud to
say. She'ld never have to sile her white
little hands with looking arter the beasts,
I'll warrant you. She could set all day
in the best parlour on the sofa and read
her book. She shud have everything she
set her heart on, and never do a stroak o'
work from morn till eve. I'm a rich
man now, Mr. Lawrance. I've nigh a
couple of hunderd acres of land as turns
me in a good fairish profit come fine
seasons and come foul. I'm not so poor
as my wife should break her back with
housework.'

'Yes, yes,' said Mr. Lawrance ; 'but
some one must look after the house!'

'There's Susie,' ventured the eager

lover, 'as knows every stock and stone in
th' old place, as 'ud be proud to stay on
and see arter the managing o' things.
I've got a little house in Wood Lane as
she cud live in with my mother, and come
backards and forrards every day, or they
cud stay on, just as Sylvie likes. No need
to think of the work, Mr. Lawrance ;
there's many an old woman in Arden as
'ud jump for joy to come and manage for
us for twelve pound a year and her keep.
There's a plenty of old women, but there's
only one Sylvie as ever I set eyes on.'

'I don't say no,' said Mr. Lawrance,
'and I don't say yes. The fact is, it is not
in the pale of my jurisdiction ; not in the
pale of—— Do you love him, Sylvie ?'

Arden started.

'Oh, Sylvie!' cried her lover, 'I doan't
ask thee to love me. Bear with me, dear,
and let me stand up for thee and take care
of thee, and have the thought and love of
thee allus in my heart. It's a great

sacrifice, Sylvie, to bid you make for the likes of me. But you're loanly, Sylvie, here, and I'm loanly; and I'ld love you true and firm till death do us part.'

'That's so long,' cried Arden, with a little shudder. 'What shall I do? What shall I say?'

'Pore child!' cried Harry. 'You look in a maze, like, with doubt and wonder. Doan't you get frabbing over me, Sylvie. I'ld like to save you trouble and not to saddle you with it. If you'ld trust me, if you'ld only trust me, I'ld so smooth and soften things for your resting on 'em. But now I'll not take up your time, Muster Lawrance. Like enough you're busy this harvesting time, only I thought it best to be plain and straightforrard.'

Arden looked on while Harry and her grandfather made their brief adieux. She did not go out to the door with Harry, but ran up to her own room. There she thought to unravel the tangled skein of her heart; but, weary and tired, she fell asleep in the straight-backed red armchair by the hearth. She slept long and deep, and dreamed sweetly—dreamed of Rome, of Gerard and Ellie, of her father, and Mr. Rose, with his thin face and hollow voice. Then she woke with a start, for she dreamed she had strayed away from her companions and was lost, alone, in the chill, grey shadow of the ilex-trees.

CHAPTER XXI.

WOO'D, MARRIED, AND A'.

It was all settled at the apple-gathering
Susie had pressed her friend to come to, so
Arden laid her doubts and fears aside, and
left the chill and narrow kindness of her
home to find light, warmth, merriment,
and welcome at the Farm. It was a beautiful September day, warm and sunny. On
the orchard that Arden had painted, the
sun shed its mellowest rays, and the grass
was all flecked and streaked with light.
There were ladders set against the trees,
and the men lying along the boughs
tumbled the red and yellow fruit into bas-
kets that the women held up beneath. It
was while Arden was holding up a great

osier basket for the apples that Harry in
the tree sent pelting down, that she determined to leave her dull, vacant home, and
make a part of this busy, happy household.
' If he should ask me again,' Arden thought ;
and before their work was finished he had
asked and she had consented.

She did not regret it that evening
when, as they all sat roasting apples round
the fire, Harry told his mother and sister.
The pride and delighted incredulity of
Mrs. Williams sweetly flattered the poor
lonely girl, who had of late grown drearily
accustomed to find herself merely a stranger in the way. And Susie flung her arms
'round her new sister's neck in a burst of
grateful affection. Harry was kind, too,
and gently considerate, asking her questions about her old foreign life, and never
plaguing her with the newer claims of his
devotion. She was left free to become at
home in her new house, simply and without demonstration. And though, when at

last she rose to leave, her cheeks were wet,
for she had been talking of her father, she
was not unhappy. It was pleasant to
belong to somebody, to have rights and
duties and a place in the world again.

She was not, indeed, 'in love' with
Harry as she had known some of her friends
to be in love. On the other hand, she
cared for him very much more than certain
other friends cared for their husbands, who
had been held to make brilliant marriages.
Arden, brought up with somewhat foreign
notions, considered herself quite sufficiently
devoted. She had a great trust in Harry;
a quiet, reliant affection. She liked him
to take care of her; it pleased her to see
the hold she had upon him; and though
she did not see him very often, she was
sorry when he went away.

Yet she certainly did not wish for an
everlasting _tête-à-tête_. She used all her
influence to persuade Mrs. Williams and
Susie to stay on in the old home. And so

it was arranged; but the best parlour,
locked up for years, was refurnished as a
special sitting-room for Arden. It was a
large, light, pleasant room on the opposite
side of the passage to the common parlour
and higher than that, for to get to it you
went up a little flight of steps. The wain-
scot was painted apple-blossom colour; the
hangings were all of white holland, and
the chairs and the new sofa were covered
with it. John Lawrance's pictures hung on
the walls; and there was a bookcase full of
books which Arden had chosen in Leamington; and her guitar hung by a red
ribbon from the wall. The windows were
filled with geraniums and fuchsias. It
looked like the bower of a bride.

A little staircase with a carved rail led
to a big bedroom above, which, like the
sitting-room, had another door leading on
to the landing; so that the occupant of
these two rooms could be sociable or re-

tired, as fancy prompted. These were to be Arden's special share of the house.

In October they were married. It was a quiet wedding, one Sunday morning before the service began. Mrs. Williams would indeed have liked to make a show—it was not every farmer's wife whose stepson connected himself with the quality!—but Arden pleaded her recent loss, and of course she had her way. So one Sunday she drove to church, with Mr. and Mrs. Lawrance, closely wrapped in furs, which left no ruching visible of the short gown of white satin underneath; and at the church door she met her bridegroom, Susie her bridesmaid, and Mrs. Williams all a flutter with ribbons and ostrich tips. Her grandfather gave her away; and scarcely did she understand the step she had taken before the brief service was over, and she was Farmer Williams' wife.

They passed down the fast-filling

church, where eager hands outstretched
from every pew greeted the bridal pair,
while hearty voices blessed them. And
every voice said something kind of Harry.
He strode down the aisle erect and proud,
with shining eyes.

' I have to keep nudging myself to feel
it's true,' he whispered to his silent little
bride.

At last the shaking of hands was done,
and the voices came to an end. Then the
little wedding procession stepped up to the
sunny churchyard. A rank of school-
children, to whom Mr. Law had given
some late roses and chrysanthemums, stood
in the porch of the church; and as the
bride and bridegroom came up the steps
from the aisle below, they threw their
flowers with a hearty will, pelting them
with sweet and bitter blossoms. One
caught in the lace at Arden's breast; it was
a blood-red chrysanthemum, fair to see,
but with the smell of wormwood.

She smiled at the children and stuck
the flower in her bodice as she stepped
out where the October sunshine lay like
palest gold over the mounded graves. It
fell, too, on her white dress and sweet,
smiling face.

' 'Appy the braïde the sun shaïnes on!'
shouted the children; and Harry pressed
the little hand that lay so lightly on his
arm.

So they were married, and all her
struggles over. At first the bird beats
wildly against the strange, confining bars,
but soon it is reconciled and makes of the
cage a home. It is true that not only
singing nightingales, but even chirping
robins, die in confinement; but there are
many more that live—linnets, canaries,
thrushes, blackbirds, even the wild and
soaring lark. So that the chances are for
happiness. And Arden surely might be
happy now that in this cold foreign land
she had found a love that was warm and

familiar, to be hers till death. Poor little
frozen bird, unable to find food or shelter
in the winter nights, surely the comfortable cage stored with grain and wool will
be a happier world for its piteous helpless-
ness!

When the wedding breakfast was over
and Harry and his bride had left the
Bushes for their honeymoon at Leamington, Susie and her mother took their leave
and walked home together. Mrs. Williams
was full of conversation. Mrs. Lawrance's
moulds and made dishes, the cut glass and
dessert knives, the Venetian decanters and
Faïence fruit dishes (which John had given
his mother years before), filled her soul
with wonder and envy. At the same time
there was an absence of solid fare which
she could not justify to herself on such an
auspicious occasion; and Susie had to listen
to many *pros* and *cons*, as she walked
wearily home. She was very tired and
still weak from her illness, and sad

thoughts of her own frustrated love would keep breaking through the talk of Harry's wedding. It was an effort to answer her mother's merry chatter; but the effort braced her heart and did her good.

'I wonder now,' said Mrs. Williams, 'where they got the notion of them chicken-patties from? They were very genteel.'

'You might ask Mrs. Lawrance,' suggested Susie.

'So I might. I suppose, the two houses being connected.' Mrs. Williams bridled a little. 'Although I can't quite say I approved of having no substantial victuals. What do you think, Susie?'

'Well, it was very early, mother dear.'

'Of course,' rejoined the elder lady. 'But in my young days—and you know I used to move in very genteel society before I married your dear papa—in my young days, as I was saying, a wedding breakfast was always quite a solid meal.'

'Perhaps the fashion's changed,' put in Susie.

'May be,' replied her mother doubtfully; 'perhaps; but what muddles me is this. One never knows, concerning the way they carry on at the Bushes, how much of it comes from Mr. Lawrance being a quality-man, and how much from his wife being a servant-like, as one might say.'

'It is puzzling, I suppose,' assented Susie. 'You might ask Sylvie which is the correct fashion.'

'Ay, so I might, Susie!' cried her mother. 'That's certain, Sylvie's a real lady—quite *distinguée*, as we used to say at school. Every inch a lady she is, the dear child.'

'And so good, too!' cried Susie; 'so sweet and kind and helpful. I'm sure I thank God every night for having sent her to us!'

'It 'ull be a comfort,' said Mrs. Williams, 'to have her always in the house.

Many's the time I've wanted some one to give me a hint about my caps and dresses.'

'I'm sure you couldn't look nicer, mother,' cried Susie, gazing with admiring eyes at the odd little flibberty-gibbet at her side.

'That's all very well,' said her mother 'but there's a different *cashy* about Sylvie's things. We shall do matters now in a very different style, and get into quite another set, no doubt.'

'We can't desert our old friends,' cried the girl.

'Who talked about desarting, Susie?' said her mother severely. 'They mustn't be presooming, that's all. I can't have the Kings and the Willises forced down Sylvie's throat.'

Susie said nothing.

'You see,' her mother went on, 'she will naterally want things done in the way she's always been accustomed to. I must give Harry a hint about his boots; 'tisn't

decent of him to come to tea so muddy.
She'll have quite a genteel influence over
him, no doubt, and I'm sure there's room
for improvement.   I'm quite longing,
Susie, as you should get married too—so
nice as we'ld manage the wedding!'

'Oh, mother,' said Susie in a hushed
hurt whisper, 'you know that can never
be!'

'And why not, I should like to know?
Now don't tell me you can't forget him—
nasty, low-minded fellow—or I shall say
you have no proper pride.   Of course I
don't mean you to marry young Warner.
I should always say No, if I was you, to
the likes of him.   But Sylvie has plenty of
acquaintances among the gentry—she said
as much herself—and a nod's as good as a
wink to a blind horse——'

Mrs. Williams gradually stopped her
harangue, conjuring up a golden future, in
which Susie was married to a foreign Count
with ardent black eyes and a thrilling tenor

voice. Mrs. Williams—who prided herself
upon her freedom from insular prejudices
—was so elated at the distinction of this
idea that she had not half exhausted its
resources when she reached her own gate.
She did not notice it and was going further
on, when Susie stopped her.

'Why, here we are, mother!' she cried.

'We shall see what we shall see,'
replied Mrs. Williams oracularly.

There was plenty to do during the
bride and bridegroom's absence; for
neither Susie nor her mother would have
been happy, had not everything in the
house shone and glistened as brightly as
they hoped their Sylvie's future might.
They gave themselves little rest from
their endeavours; washing all the pret-
tiest, long-treasured china for Arden's
rooms, and filling the bowls with pot-
pourri; transferring all her treasures from
the Bushes to her new home; unpack-
ing her things, and laying them neatly

in her drawers, between sprigs of lemon-
plant and lavender, that she might find
all ready to her hand, and feel herself
indeed at home. There was great business
in the kitchen, also : plum-puddings and
mincemeat to make, and a grand baking
of cakes and dainties. When the last day
of the honeymoon was over, there was
still so much to finish that Susie rose
long, long before the wintering sun began
to shine. A final polish was given to
all the brass and woodwork, a final
daintiness to Arden's quarters ; the few
rare flowers that grew in the sheltered
kitchen window were plucked and put
in water on her table ; immense fires
blazed in the grates ; the easiest chair
was drawn to the hearth. At last, the
spring-cart was sent to the station ; it
would hold but two, so Curtis was de-
spatched with it, with orders to walk
home ; and then, there being no speck
or dimness left throughout the house,

Susie and her mother went upstairs to
make themselves as orderly. Susie, even,
had scarcely finished her swift adornment,
before she spied the cart coming down
the lane, at a great pace. 'How glad
they are to get home!' she cried. In
another moment, the whole household was
at the door.

'Welcome, my daughter Sylvie!' cried
little Mrs. Williams, with tears in her
eyes. The cart stopped; Harry sprang
down, and lifted out his bride. But
could that be Sylvie—that pale, listless,
weary girl, who smiled wanly at them,
and walked, without a word of thanks,
into the room they had made so beautiful for her? She sank into the great
chair with a weary sigh; and they all
stood looking at her—Harry, beseeching
and hurt; Mrs. Williams, amazed past all
belief; Susie, with tender kindness and
concern. But Arden did not look up.
'Oh, I am so tired!' she sighed at last;

and her head fell back against the chair.
Susie came forward quietly. 'That's it,'
she cried; 'she's tired out. Go away,
you foolish people, and get her some
tea, instead of wanting to kiss her. I'll
see to that.'

'La, Susie!' ejaculated Mrs. Williams;
but she took Harry's arm, and walked out
of the door which Susie held open for
them with a show of mock imperious-
ness. But, once the door was shut, the
girl dropped her pretty airs, and ran to
Arden's side.

'What is it, my darling—what have
they done to you, my sweet Princess
Sylvie?' she cried, as she dropped on
her knees by the chair and took Arden's cold hands in hers.

Arden opened her eyes, and smiled.

'Dear Susie!' she said.

'What is it, darling?' implored the
younger girl. 'Are you ill? or—unhappy?'

Arden stooped forward, and leant her head on Susie's shoulder.

'Oh, yes,' she cried, 'I am miserably unhappy. Why didn't you—why did not some one—let me know what I was doing? I can't live, Susie; I'm sick of life—it's hateful!'

'What, Harry?' cried his sister. 'Is he bad to you—Harry?'

'Oh, no, he's good enough,' said the young bride, wearily; 'too good, I think; only I am so tired of it all—so very, very tired.'

She stopped for a little while. 'And I am only seventeen,' she went on; 'so young! How could I know what it all meant? I have been so much alone; I've never had a sister, or even a friend all of my own. How could I know, Susie, what it would be like to have some one always there, day and night, no place to call one's own? To be, soul and body, always in sight of some

one else—always to be watched, looked at,
talked to, kissed—oh, I have longed, longed
to be alone, for just one hour, and I couldn't
have it ; if I said a word, he looked so
grieved! And I don't want to grieve
him, you know, Susie. I do love him :
only it kills me to belong to him.'

'Sylvie!' cried the other girl. 'Oh,
I don't know what you mean! There
must be something behind.'

'And I'm so young!' moaned Arden,
wearily ; 'it may go on for years, and
years, and years.' The tears, the young
sweet-sour tears of self-pity, escaped from
her closed lids and fell on to her hands.

CHAPTER XXII.

NEEDLES AND PINS.

SUSIE persuaded her mother and Harry that nothing ailed the poor little bride, beyond some natural nervousness, and an excessive fatigue. They were very kind to her, hiding their disappointment under renewed efforts to please her; and Arden tried her best to be grateful. But there was a change in her, not to be disguised. Week by week, she grew frailer and paler, and her fresh little face became quite wan and drawn. She was, however, the least presuming of daughters-in-law, never claiming any share in the ordering of the house, which she left entirely in Susie's capable hands. She quite fulfilled

Harry's promises, and sat on the sofa in her parlour all day long, reading a book over the fire. Susie took care that she should have time to herself, and without a word managed to divert Mrs. Williams from her plans of always leaving some one to keep Arden company. And so, for many hours a day, Arden might, if she chose, read or dream alone, as she had done in the old days. But in the old days the winters were not so cold and dreary, and the girl herself had not always felt so tired, so nervous, so old, so deathly sick. When the new year came round, you would not have recognised, in that pale, drawn woman, lying back, with closed eyes, the pretty girl who had looked so happy and shy at the apple-gathering. But the little household at the Farm looked at her with proud and loving eyes.

' She will be all right, now !' cried Mrs. Williams, nodding mysteriously. And

Harry's great love of her grew stronger than of old, swollen by fresh tides of tenderness and compunction.

Arden was to be a mother : that happy secret made a new gladness in every heart round the great fireside on winter evenings. But Arden herself, lying a little apart on the easiest couch, did not feel very glad. She was so ill, poor child : it seemed that there would be no end to these weary, restless nights, the sickening waking, the exhausted days. And she had a great dread of the future. Sometimes, nevertheless, she brooded tenderly over the sweet new life that should belong to her—should satisfy her, and answer all the longings of her heart ; and at such times her weariness seemed a little price to pay. But they were not very frequent, these maternal impulses. Arden was not eighteen herself. It is older mothers who love their children most.

The sad, long winter dragged away, the frosty ground grew soft with February showers, the spurge-laurel broke into flower under the firs on the other side of the lane, and the deep snow melted off the pasture-lands; the cattle and the herds, long pent-up from the cold, were driven out again to grass, whisking their tails in the air, and bounding gladly, though their coats were rough and shaggy and they had lost their comfortable roundness. For since mid-December the snow had lain thick and white upon the ground, and the beasts in their dark stalls and folds had lived off dry hay and roots.

The spring was early that year, and by March the grass sprang green and fresh in the meadows, and daisies and primroses began to lift their starry heads on every bank and ridge. The buds were swelling on the bushes, though the trees were bare, or only brushed at

the tops with a faint, promising red.
The blackthorn was white in the hedges,
the birds began to twitter, the sky cleared
and lightened, fresh and blue, above the
fresh greening world. The commons were
a blaze of yellow gorse. Flowers springing everywhere, birds crying and calling,
sunlight and sweet air, all showed the
spring was here. And by the kitchen
fire the weakest of the weanling lambs
lay in its warm basket: every few days.
Susie would bring into Arden's parlour.
a flannel-covered hamper, where yellow
downy chickens pecked and chirped. It
was impossible to feel very miserable, in
the midst of all this new, springing life:
and Arden grew gay and loving as of
old, taking the little lamb for walks up
and down the passages, and feeding the
chickens with sopped bread and beer.
Perhaps it was not good for the lamb
to be kept trotting about on the stone
floors; and some of the fledglings cer-

tainly died from over-feeding ; but no
one would have dreamed of crossing
Arden's fancy for them. It was so pleasant, so relieving to see her look bright
and natural again.

'I've been in the house three months!'
she said, one day, with a sigh. 'I should
like to go out again, Harry, when you've
got through with your sowing and
ploughing.'

'Woo't have me drive thee to-day to
Farley Common ?' cried Harry, overjoyed
(although last year he would not have
left the 'Five Acre' to Curtis's tender
mercies, for any woman alive). 'It's fair
glorious upon the common, now, with
the sky so blue, and the skylarks singing
in it, and the gorse out in bloom, in the
likeness of a sheet of gold.'

'Oh, I should like to go,' said Arden,
'if you'd care to take me!'

'That would I, my darling,' cried her
husband, as he came round and kissed

her. It made him so happy to serve
her, when she would let him, and it was
sweet to see the flush of pleasure in her
pale cheeks again. Arden leant her head
against his shoulder.

'I'm so glad the spring has come,
Harry,' she said; 'something tells me
we're going to be happy now.'

'I'm happy, Sylvie, winter and spring
alike, whatever befall us, if thou'rt by my
side, and out of pain.'

'Dear Harry!' said Arden, stroking
one of his hands.

'Thou'rt easier, to-day, I fancy, love?'

'Oh, yes,' said Arden; 'well and
contented, and in a good temper, for
once.'

She laughed a quick little laugh, and
with a sudden movement dragged down
her husband's shock head with both her
hands. 'You love your cross old wife,
don't you?' she said; and looked at
him with tender mockery. But she set

him free without the kiss he had hoped
for.

'We're quite old married people, now,'
she said, as if in excuse.

'Ay, Sylvie, so it is. How can I
thank you, darling, for all thou'st done
for me? My happiness, my love! before
I had thee I was often lonely, even with
the little 'un allus after me. But now,
Sylvie, there's not an empty cranny in
my heart. 'Tis right full of thee, my
girl; and all my days are full; so that,
if I'm busy with the sowing, I think
only of how thou'lt like to look at the
harvest; and I look for the apple-blossom
more than the fruit, 'cause you'll want
to paint it, you said. And I declare if
I don't think more o' the lambs than
the yows, since you've taken a fancy
to have them foller you about. See
what a fool thou'st got for a husband,
Sylvie!'

'Then you've been quite satisfied,

Harry ? ' she said, with a wondering query in her voice. ' You've been happy, all these months ? '

' Oh, my love, I never rightly knew what 'twas to be happy afore ! '

' I'm glad,' she said ; and then kept silence, wondering.

Arden went out that afternoon for her first drive. Tender hands wrapped her round and placed soft cushions at her back ; but their care was all in vain. Over Farley Common the sky suddenly grew black, and the sun beat luridly upon the golden gorse. The air was still—the birds sang over-loud. Arden had alighted to pluck some primroses, and, deaf to Harry's warning, would not believe in the storm to come. She looked very pretty and wayward, with her hands full of flowers.

' But love, Sylvie,' cried Harry, ' I tell 'ee the storm's gathering overhead.'

' Look at the sun !' cried Arden ; 'what

nonsense! It's only because you want to get me in.'

'Well, then, dear,' pleaded her husband, at his wits' end, 'woo't get into the cart to do me a pleasure, storm or no storm.'

'Not I!' cried Arden. 'I think it's very selfish of you to plague me so.'

'Selfish, Sylvie?' said Harry, quite bewildered.

'*Altro!* It's the first time I've enjoyed myself for months!'

'Well,' cried Harry, heroically, 'say I'm a beast—but come.'

'In a moment,' said Arden calmly, and went on gathering her posy.

Harry stood and looked at her, utterly helpless. She was going further away from the cart towards a little stream whereby some lady-smocks were lilac already. As she went, she hummed to herself an airy Italian song. She seemed in no hurry. Harry would have liked to pick her up in his arms and carry her away, but he was afraid of hurting her. She was, in fact, quite unassailable.

'Come, Sylvie, love,' said Harry in despair.

'Oh, what lovely lilies!' cried Arden, and stretched out her hands to gather the delicate white cups and rank odour of the wild garlic.

At that moment a brilliant flash of lightning ran across the common. In a minute the thunder pealed. Arden hurried to her husband. 'I'll come now, Harry,' she said, dropping her malodorous lilies, and clung to his arm like a frightened child. But it was too late. The rain fell in drenching sheets ; before they reached the tethered cart they were both wet to the skin, and there was a five-mile drive before them. Before Arden reached home she was very ill, and for many days after that she lay in danger of her very life. So much was saved by skill and loving care, but when at last they carried her downstairs to

lie again on the sofa in her blossom-
coloured parlour, they knew that the hope
of many months was dead. No child would
be born with the roses to fill the wide old
house with life and mirth.

CHAPTER XXIII.

OLD FRIENDS.

ONE warm April evening, Arden, filled with the restlessness of Spring, slid away from the busy circle by the fireside, and, seizing her gardening cloak and hat, went out into the quiet garden. She had often done so of late ; for sometimes, when Harry and his sister were settling the affairs of the Farm, while Mrs. Williams dozed in her chair, a terrible sense of isolation would rush over this married child, and make her long to be indeed alone. Then she would escape into the quiet night, where the white flowers in the borders trembled dimly through the dark, and the trees were tall and dim, and the air blue above. She would pace to and fro here, calmly, till the vague yearning in her soul was soothed to rest.

But to-night there was no such dimness. The full moon lit up the furthest spaces of the clear blue sky; the stars alone were dim and flickered; all the earth lay broad and calm, washed in the pale greenish light. One could see so far, and the wide valley looked so fair that Arden did not care to linger in the garden; she loosed the watch-dog in the yard, and, wrapping her long cloak round her, she passed through the gate on to the broad white road, barred here and there with the fantastic elm-tree shadows.

How beautiful the view would be from the rise beyond the canal bridge! From there one could see in broadest day a landscape always edged with dim blue misty woods—so far could one look. And in this unearthly light the scene would indeed be strange and fair; so Arden, with Tory at her side, set bravely forth, a little wondering at her own venturesomeness, although the dangers that she ran were not appalling, for the hill was scarcely a ten minutes' walk away, and her road lay through the straggling village street.

She reached the rise, and stood to look upon the view. It was a wonderful and vague expanse, trembling in the wan light of the April morn—every detail, clear but thin, and, as it were, in profile. Fair as the valley was, the sky was fairer and more necessary to the scene ; it looked as deep, and clear, and greenly blue as the still spaces of a waveless sea ; and on its surface of untroubled calm, flecks of foamy cloud were splashed in airy lightness.

Arden stood and gazed, leaning against a gate. The wonderful sight took all the trouble from her soul ; it was too fair to leave at once, and yet too cold to stop still. So she walked a little way further on, descending the hill on the other side, promising herself one final view from the summit, when, in a few minutes, she should turn back for home.

She herself, wandering swiftly in her dark cloak and grey dress, singing under her breath, appeared some fairy denizen of the moonlight as she flitted softly down the hill.

In the bottom, further down the lane, a young man was standing where three roads met, looking at the sign-post, almost defaced by the showers of many winters. 'To Raynham,' was clear on one of the arms, 'Clin——' was still discernible on the other, but the one which pointed ahead was past all deciphering.

'Well, it can't be Raynham, and it can't be Clin——' said Gerard Rose. 'I'll chance the other one.'

So he strode straight forwards up the rise. He walked quickly on, looking to right and left ; at last he neared the top.

He stood for a moment and looked at the beautiful night.

'I presume there's an inn where I can sleep for the night. It looks a quiet, peaceful place. Dear little Arden!'

The young man, as he spoke, moved out of the shadow of the hedge in which he had been standing, and came into the light of the road. Suddenly a weak cry caught his ear, and at the same moment he perceived a shadowy outline, familiar and strange at once, standing in front of him.

'Arden!' he cried, in some alarm.

'Oh, Gerard, is it you? I was so frightened! How did you come? I thought you were in Syria.'

'Evidently not,' said Gerard; 'but, my dear child, how can they let you roam about alone at this time of night? It's very wrong.'

'They don't know I'm out,' cried Arden. 'Oh, they'll be so glad to see you! I've often talked of you.'

Gerard looked at her. 'So you're happy?' he said, with a query in his voice.

'Oh, yes. You must come home with me. You can't think what a beautiful home I've got. *Mais d'un caractère!* You'll be sketching it all day long.'

'Is that so?' said Gerard, a little surprised, for she had never seemed enraptured with the Bushes in her letters. 'But I guess I want to hear about you, Arden dear, not the house.'

'Oh, I'm all right,' said Arden; 'at least, I've been very ill. How is Mrs. Rose?'

'Ill, Arden? And they allow you—— Anyhow, it's an impossibility that you should continue here.'

'How cross you are!' said Arden. 'You might put it off until you've seen me a little longer. Oh, Gerard, it is so nice to see you again!'

'It's very "nice" to hear you say so,

every time,' said Gerard, gazing at her a
little wistfully.

They were now at the bridge.

' How beautiful it is in this sweet light!'
said Gerard. ' Like a forgotten page out of
Shakespeare's comedies.'

' That's the house,' cried Arden ; 'that
black and white one, among the apple-
trees. And, oh, Gerard, you mustn't be
surprised if he's not quite the sort of
person you expected to see. Really, you
know, he's of a much older family than
mine, and they've lived in that house
three hundred years. And he's so good
and kind.'

' A much older family than yours?'
cried Gerard, in his old, gay, mocking voice.
' Of course I know you're quite a special
person, Arden; but, my dear girl, do tell me
how one's grandfather, even yours——'

Arden began to laugh. ' Oh, you silly
boy!' she cried. ' It's not grandpapa ; it's
Harry.'

Gerard stared at her in dumb surprise, suddenly chill and afraid.

'Didn't you get my letter?' cried Arden. 'Oh, you haven't been to Beyrout?'

Gerard shook his head.

'And you don't know?' went on Arden, rather frightened. 'Oh, Gerard, I'm married!'

For a moment the young man said nothing; he was cruelly taken aback. But the strong desire not to show Arden how deeply he was moved, helped him to keep under his anger and amazement.

'You must own it is rather a surprise!' he exclaimed.

'Yes,' said Arden. 'But come and let me show him to you. He's only a farmer, you know, Gerard.'

'Indeed!'

It was a night of surprises, certainly. Gerard felt a bitter conviction forced upon him that, however brutal the Beast might be, Beauty would find no difficulty in marrying him if there were no one else in view. But it was too bad of Arden; she must have known he cared for her.

Arden suddenly stopped.

'You're not one bit nice, Gerard!' she cried; 'you've not wished me joy or said one single kind thing. Are you ashamed of me because I've married a farmer?'

'Why no, Arden, dear,' said the young man, not without an effort. 'Only it requires more ingenuity than I possess to say kind things about a man whom I have never seen and have only heard of as "Harry," in a vague sort of way; but I'm sure he's an excellent fellow, or you would never have married him. I guess we can get along,' he added, more generously.

'Thank you, Gerard,' said Arden; 'oh, how is Miss De la Rue?'

'Miss De la Rue!' cried Gerard, amazed, 'I believe she's dying, poor girl. But how on earth did you hear of her?'

' Ellie told me,' said Arden, with a voice of profoundest sympathy.

' Told you what?' cried the other, as a dim light began to break on his mind. ' Little mischief - maker! You didn't believe her, Arden? You didn't think I could care for her? But are you going to take me in with you, Arden?'

' Of course,' she said ; ' you are to stay with us. It is so nice to have a home of one's own ! '

The door was open in the fearless country fashion, and, taking Gerard by the hand, she led him down the queer little passage, always breaking into flights of steps, into her blossom-coloured parlour. She left him there, and ran into the other room, where Mrs. Williams was still dozing, Susie and Harry still doing accounts, as if no great event had surprised the world since Arden left them.

' Harry,' she cried, in a quick, eager

voice, 'the most wonderful thing has happened!'

Harry looked at her. Never since he had first seen her swinging the honeysuckle trails as she walked singing down the lane, had he seen her look so gay, so young, so fair. Her eyes danced and sparkled, her lips curled up in the charming, youthful smile of a faun; she looked the very incarnation of careless love.

'Well, and whatever it be, I'm glad of it, Sylvie,' said her husband; 'you look quite your old self again, so pleasant like and well.'

'Dear old Harry!' cried Arden; 'but you'll never guess; I may as well tell you. Gerard's here!'

'Gerard!' said Harry, uneasily. He seemed to hear again the dull flap of the yellow blind against the chemist's window, to see the dim lighted room, and Arden's senseless face.

'Why, certainly,' cried Arden. 'Have

you forgotten all the times I've told you about him—my friend, who used to play with me when I was a little girl?—and you don't remember!' There were infinite reproaches in her voice.

'Yes, dearie, I remember,' cried Harry. 'I'm fair glad he's come since thou'rt so pleased to see him. Thou'st not left him in the lane?'

'No,' cried Arden, 'he's in the parlour. Oh, Harry, I am so happy and pleased!'

'And so am I, then, darling.'

'Here he is,' said Arden, as they came into the pretty white room. She went in first and Harry followed her, wearing a sheepish rustic simper of embarrassment. Gerard came forward with his handsome, nonchalant air. He stood before Arden with his fine smile, waiting for her to speak.

'Gerard,' said Arden, suddenly a little grave, 'this is my husband!'

CHAPTER XXIV.

TWO'S COMPANY.

MRS. WILLIAMS was almost as pleased as
Arden that Gerard should stay at the Farm;
but she had the unusual good sense to keep
to herself the plans that her motherly
mind matured regarding him and Susie.
'A nice pleasant-spoken young gentleman,'
she called him once to her daughter, 'far
more genteel than that worthless young
Masters.' But Susie's reddening cheek
and flashing eye warned off this enthusiasm
for comparison.

As for Gerard he troubled himself very
little about the yellow-haired Susie. He
felt, all the time that he acknowledged their
kindness and worth, a certain irritation

against these underbred, respectable,
countrified people, who had deprived him
of Arden in the very moment when, after
much painful hesitation, he had resolved
to throw prudence to the winds and marry
her. He had never even dreamed that in the
meantime she would marry another man ;
and that his successful rival should be a
mere good-humoured lout of a farmer, was
a galling addition to his grievance.

Nevertheless he permitted the good-
humoured lout to continue his host,
although a dozen times a day he reproached
himself with the fact. But it was not
easy to get away; for Williams pressed
the new comer to remain, being anxious
to please his little wife, who had recovered
her old gay spirits since Gerard's arrival.
Harry, for his part, was not vain, and saw
no reason why his wife should not have
been 'moped' in her dull quiet life with
him, nor why the excitement of seeing an
old friend should not dispel her melan-

choly. So with cordial hospitality he pressed
Gerard to stay for a while. And Arden
herself was so pleased, so eager, so merry :
taking Gerard over all her premises, explor-
ing barns, fowl pens, hay lofts, stables, folds,
like a happy child. It would certainly be
difficult to leave her, thought the young
man. And, after all, no one guessed that he
had come as her lover, not merely as her
friend. There was no harm done to any
but himself by that blunder, reasoned
Gerard. He had accepted the situation,
so he stayed on.

It must be owned that after the first
few days Gerard's visit became a veritable
trial to the slower witted farmer. Unable
to retaliate, but conscious of an indefin-
able, unseizable antagonism at work ; he
was always being made to feel his own
inferiority, always being reminded that he
was a new comer in Arden's life. From
all their reminiscences he was naturally
shut out. Sometimes it flashed across him

how unfit he was for the refined, graceful, delicate young girl at his side. He and Susie, she and Gerard, seemed the denizens of different spheres.

And indeed it was plain that Gerard thought the same. He did not mean to goad and torture the unhappy man, who every day felt himself sinking further and further below the level of his bride. He believed that the farmer did not understand the little half allusions with which he pointed the difference between them ; but, in truth, it was Arden who did not understand ; not a syllable was lost upon her husband.

Nevertheless Harry held his peace for Arden's sake, and even assented to half her praise of Gerard. Thank Heaven, it was impossible to suspect her guileless, gentle nature ; she seemed more than ever sweet, more than ever undeserved, to Harry in her innocent gaiety, her childish eager-ness to make her friend and her husband each admire the other. Harry would not for worlds have darkened her pretty, simple happiness.

Nevertheless it was bitter to think how recently his love had touched her. 'Do you remember?' Gerard would begin, and Arden's eyes would flash and the colour strike up her cheek; now he could never make her look so glad. Yet he was glad to see her happy; he could not (he kept saying to himself) be such a fool as to be jealous, for the dear little girl was more loving and kind to him than she had ever been before. Her nature seemed to expand in happiness, like a pimpernel in the sun. Indeed, these were very happy days to Arden, who never dreamed that Gerard could have thought of her with lover's love, nor deemed it possible that her husband could be jealous of Gerard.

One fine evening they were all sitting in the wainscoted parlour, and while Susie sang an air of Handel's, Gerard was turning

her pages; Mrs. Williams stopped her
talking to gaze at them with eyes of pride;
and Arden and her husband, seated in the
settle, talked in hushed voices not to mar
the music. Susie had a fine voice, but she
sang without style and dragged the time;
so that to Gerard's fastidious ear her per-
formance was a pleasure much alloyed.
When he had finished thanking her and
pointing out one or two *fioriture* which she
might alter, Susie conscientiously sat down
and tried the air again, as though he had
been giving her a music lesson. Gerard,
who wanted to talk to Arden, stood by her
side listening with a sort of careless weariness; and while he was standing so, his
eyes fell on the settle where Arden, with a
bewitching pout, was lifting her arm to her
husband to show a long scratch that the
kitten had made. Harry stooped down
and kissed the wounded wrist, saying
something to his wife that made her laugh
and lift her blue eyes to his face. It

was a pretty, harmless little scene ; but it filled Gerard with uncontrollable aversion. He longed to get Arden away, to have her to himself. Just then Susie finished.

'Bravo!' said Gerard hurriedly; 'that's much better, Miss Susie. Arden, I guess it's your turn now to come and warble.'

'Ay go, Sylvie love,' said her husband ; 'thou'st forgotten thy singing of late.'

'I'm so comfortable,' said Arden lazily.

'Do come, Arden !' implored Gerard.

'It sounds so strange-like,' said the farmer, with a slow amused smile, 'to hear my wife called by her fust name. 'Tis the name of the village, you know, Mr. Rose.'

'I know,' said Gerard, 'but her old friends always called her so.'

Harry's face darkened. It was not a fortunate speech.

'I'll sing, if Harry wants me to sing,' said Arden. 'Gerard, what shall my song be to-night?'

'Sing me a song of Zion!' said the

young man. He had seated himself on the other side of her, with his arms crossed behind his head, in the corner of the settle. He looked at her.

'A hymn!' cried Susie, with round eyes.

'No, Miss Susie; I mean the other Holy City: Rome, the Eternal.'

'Shall I sing,' said Arden, 'that song the Saracen pedlars used to sing? Don't you remember when Ellie was photographed as one of those women, and I cried so because Papa wouldn't let me be done too!'

'You were nine years old then,' said Gerard.

'And you a year older. I used to think you so clever!'

'*Grazie* for the past tense! You're through with that delusion now, I presume.'

They both began to laugh, and though Arden's hand was on his arm, Harry on the further side of her began very painfully to realise that only two are company.

'Sing,' went on the young man, 'a certain song you used to know—but you must fetch your guitar!—that always seems to me the most magical thing in the world. It's Venice!' Arden shuddered, but the speaker was too engrossed with his simile to notice. He went on : 'The shady spaces of the empty vestibules we look into as we pass, and the silent women with long black shawls draping their heads and shoulders, and then beyond the cool monotony of sky and lagoon, where the quietness and lap of the waters seem another tone of the universal greyness. It's all in that song!' He began to hum it *sotto voce*.

'Oh, Gerard,' cried Arden, with tears in her voice, 'you shouldn't speak to me of Venice!'

She turned away her head and laid it on her husband's shoulder.

'Miss Susie,' said Gerard, with a despairing blandness, 'I guess I want you to sing " Despised and rejected."'

Mrs. Williams smiled through her doze.

The long evening dragged itself wearily
away, but the next morning Arden came
down to breakfast singing.

'It will be my birthday on Saturday,'
she cried. 'I shall be eighteen!'

'Woot' like to give a party, Sylvie?'
said her husband.

'There's no one to ask but grandpapa
and Mrs. Lawrance. No; that would not
be very gay—but I don't want to be gay.'

'Why, Sylvie, what a sigh! Thou's
never growing melancholy, to be so old !'
said Harry.

But Gerard was looking at her with
comprehending eyes.

'I understand,' he said, in a low tone of
sympathy. 'Anniversaries are cruel days.
No,' he added rather louder for Harry's
benefit, 'we won't keep your birthday,
Arden. One doesn't feel much like ex-
posing one's birthday at such decrepitude
as that, Mr. Williams.'

The farmer chuckled slowly. 'That's
a good 'un.' he said, 'that is.'

Gerard looked at Arden. 'Then that's fixed,' he said; 'we don't celebrate your birthday. Now, Mr. Williams, let us give our manly energies the task of finding out the surest way to hide that shameful fact. As for me, I don't begin to have a first idea!' but the moment after, while Harry was still chuckling over his fantastic spirits, the young fellow added—

'I have it. Let's go to Stratford-on-Avon!'

'Done,' said Harry, 'that 'ull be a good thing over. 'T'wur too wet to go theer when we wur at Leamington.'

'I know,' said Gerard quickly : he certainly did not want to revisit the scenes of their honeymoon with the bride and bridegroom.

'Oh, Gerard! how nice of you to think of it!' cried Arden. 'I've so often wanted to go!'

'I wish I'ld ha' thought of it,' said Harry meditatively; 'but what with th' yows failing, and the ploughing, and one thing and another, I've been that mazed and muddled I cud think of nothing but worries.'

And I've been so ill, too, poor old man!' said Arden.

' Ay, that's what I meant,' said Harry gratefully. ' Thou knows I doan't care much for aught else.'

' Well, I imagine I had better go upstairs and write some letters,' said Gerard, pulling out his watch. He was a little sore that when he had made the suggestion, Harry by some feminine juggle should get the credit of it. Something of this feeling inspired the note which he went to write.

' Dear Ellie,' it began—' it is now a fortnight since I encountered Arden in the lane and was borne off to her rustic home. Certainly it is very rustic, and experience teaches that while rusticity in a house is charming, the same quality as a personal adjunct is apt to pall. As a finality, I don't believe it would wear. These remarks may be taken as applying to the family Williams, who are as excellent boors as this land of beer and fog has yet turned out. It is very odd to see Arden in the midst of them ; she has not yet found out their boorishness, and takes all their pretensions *au grand sérieux*. It appears to me they have a good many pretensions. The mother is a fussy old woman in a cap, who aspires to be genteel. The daughter is a serious prig, who dresses like a second-girl and aspires to Girton. As for the farmer, he has aspired so much in marrying Arden, that there is no need for him to do more than remain *le mari de Madame*. I find these people an interesting study. Their life is very narrow, very local, and they take it very much in earnest. But you must not suppose a New England earnestness. This is more material, and infinitely little concerned with the religious life. The soul, like the mind, does not exist for these prosperous country people.

'None the less there is a certain shrewdness, as distinct from ideas, under their well-nourished and dominant physique. The daughter, in particular, engages my attention. She has, I am certain, a character of no common type. There is, in her manner of turning all her fugitive and futile scraps of learning to account, a wisdom and *aplomb* one does not expect in a three-century farmhouse. Evidently she distrusts me. Sometimes, when I catch the serious gaze of her greenish, very steadfast eyes stealthily fixed upon me, I feel like shuddering. *Elle est capable de tout !* One can imagine her marching straight to her purposed end, unembarrassed by a single passion, a single pang. So much flashes out in a glance now and then ; else she is a girlish, countrified, slim, and rosy creature. For her portrait, imagine Becky Sharp or Emma Bovary at sixteen. This, of course, is as she exists *in posse*; *in esse* she remains an undeveloped child. I have, however, heard of an affair with the Squire's son which for rapacious passion and cool ingenuity surpasses either prototype. Frankly, you perceive I return the compliment of her distrust.

'Arden's girlish friendship for this cold and singular *Erscheinung* has for me the fascination of that other tragic spectacle, the bird charmed by the venomous snake. Joconde herself, I believe, is not more chill, more potent, more deadly in her serpentine magic than this inexperienced Susie Williams. Life is rich in possibilities. It is these which the true artist should apprehend and immortalise. In crude reality, the possible is often disregarded. This girl, with her capabilities for infinite crime, and triumph, and influence, may doubtless marry a vulgar farmer and become a vulgar shrew. Oh, for an hour of Balzac, to seize the moment and develop it; to reveal her character in its potentiality and astonish the world with the actual realisation of the dormant evil! But Balzac is dead. Seriously, Ellie, it has occurred to me that my real sphere lies not in painting, not in a mere capture of impressions, but in the penetration of character. Sometimes I feel the divining rod twitch and jerk in my grasp.

'So much of the sister, for whom, by the way, it is clear that Mrs. Williams designs your honoured brother. There is a not unpathetic comedy in the situation. This girl, afraid of me, perceiving my grasp of her dubious past, my insight into her possibly atrocious future, doing therefore her best to conciliate me; I, interested in this problematic soul, pursuing it with ruthless penetration, plucking the heart from its mystery. Meanwhile, the old fussy, vulgar mother, sits smiling and nodding in the background, ready at any moment to weep, and smile, and cry, " Bless you, my children ! "

'As for the farmer himself, he is an honest lout, a worthy boor whose soul is buried in his turnip fields, five fathom deep and more. He is evidently immensely relieved by my presence; it saves him the trouble of amusing his fine lady bride. I do not think he cares much for Arden. With that sort of man, passion is fierce but brief. Now that he is sure of her, he disregards her. Nevertheless, his narrow soul is honest, placid, incapable of resentment. He regards you with the same slow glance of amiable suspicion that his cattle lift from their pastures at the noise of your presence. Under his buffalo hide of sluggish apathy, impenetrable to the keenest darts, there exists a heart, shrivelled but kindly. I like the farmer, *per se*, but as Arden's husband I deplore him.

'As yet the revelation has not dawned. She has not yet found out that she is dying of ennui. She is still the same as

ever. wonderfully " pretty-appearing," as
they say at home, and with more charm
than any other girl begins to have. There
is a sweet incongruity in her happiness,
for I fancy she is happy. I could, at
times, believe her to be dead in love with
him. It takes so little to satisfy a woman ;
give her any husband, any children, she is
sure to love them ; their character is a
matter of detail. This, at least, is true of
the Teuton woman. Perhaps it is not
true of our finer and more nervous
race.

'So you see, dear Ellie, there was no
need of your elaborate warning. I guess I
shall get along very well with the farmer,
though I must allow his stamp of character
is a little too much *toujours rosbif.* I
believe he considers mine *toujours soufflée.*
This is an obstacle to perfect mutual com-
prehension. But as for Arden, I am not
going to make love to her. Poor child,
I care for her too well to wish to hasten

the day of apocalypse which surely must arrive. And I am not likely to ruin my career by a hopeless and guilty passion. After all, you know, I am from Boston, not a mere *boulevardier*.

'I am truly sorry to hear poor Nellie is so much worse. Give my best regards to her and to Colonel De la Rue. It is a pleasure to hear that the Mater is so much better in Cannes. I shall have finished my painting in a few more weeks, and then, if you feel like meeting me in Paris, we will have a good time there together before returning to the Riviera. Does that idea smile on you ? If you are pleased, show your gratitude by being very lovely to poor Nellie.

'Well, good-bye, my dear El; I shall see you before long.

'Believe me, not a tragic villain,

'But your affectionate,

'GERARD.

N 2

'P.S.—You need not be alarmed at
the Borgia Miss Susie ; the portrait is
perhaps a little " heightened " (as we said
in Boston), for literary purposes. I guess
we shall fix it along together.'

CHAPTER XXV.

STRATFORD-ON-AVON.

GERARD took rooms at the inn, so as to be freer for his painting ; but, nevertheless, he was continually in and out of the Farm. He and Susie became excellent friends, and had many a laugh over such details of his Borgia conception of her as he chose to impart ; but generally they spoke of Arden, on the rare occasions when she did not make a third in their merry banter. Gerard and Arden were indeed constantly together. He took her long drives in the spring cart, which left her rosy and fresh ; and she painted at his side from the same point of view. They were such old friends, and so soon to part, that they thought the time wasted which they did not spend together ; not that Arden would have chosen to neglect her husband, but the farmer was just now overworked with the first flush of his hay harvest. He could only spare a hurried moment for breakfast and supper, dining in the hay field, so that Arden had plenty of leisure to bestow on Gerard.

The village, unused to this American liberty, formed its own opinions, and these were as scandalous as village gossip can suggest. But the household at the Farm was ignorant of these evil tongues. Mrs. Williams, Susie, Arden, and Gerard were a very merry and innocent party. And Harry, too, tried to be gay, though a sudden overmastering jealousy would sometimes choke his throat and seem to stop his heart.

But though he was jealous, Harry would not for the world have let Arden guess his misery. He did not suspect her

of any one disloyal thought. He knew her
to be true and good. But he remembered
the pallid ailing wife whom he had striven
in vain to cheer, and he looked on this gay
fresh girl who enjoyed her life so well since
Gerard had come. He had done her, so
he would think, a grievous wrong in
marrying her, who could never really love
him. And then the sight of her merry
face would pacify him. ' Let her be happy
if she can, poor child,' he would think ;
and notwithstanding his secret anxiety he
could not resist a hopeful mood. She was
certainly happy now. Would she be happy
still when Gerard had left ? Such was
the problem, fraught with despair and
rapture, which haunted him by day and
night. What would the answer be ?
Sometimes it seemed so clear that his wife
had learned to love him at last, that Harry
took the answer for spoken ; and then he
would be very happy. Then he would
gladly upbraid himself for his jealous

fancies. It was a sin to suppose the most
innocent error in such a spotless life.
Arden was his, only his! Let her give
the overflowings and remnants of her love
to whom she would.

But alas! sometimes, suddenly, unaccountably, this happy assurance would
fail. He would look at his wife's pale
face and reproach himself bitterly for
having brought upon her a trouble that
she did not comprehend; or she would
sigh over some remembrance to which he
had no clue; or she and Gerard would
laugh at some allusion he could not guess.
They were always laughing at things he
could not understand! It might be they
laughed at him, too!

'Are you tired, poor old man?' Arden
would say, and come and lay her arms
on his shoulders, stooping to look at his
face. Then, at her pretty solicitude, the
frown would relax; he would love her
more than ever.

Arden's birthday morning dawned bright and clear. It was the 12th of June. All the wild roses were full in blow, and the streams smelt of the meadowsweet and willowherb upon their banks. The summer was early, and the dryest pastures were already cut for hay. They might have begun to mow the low-lying meadows, and in secret Harry's right arm longed to be sweeping the scythe through the flower-grown grass. But it was Arden's birthday, and her wish was doubly law.

They set out for Stratford by the morning train, four young people, Mrs. Williams having elected to stay and get their supper ready. Arden was so eager and delighted that her husband reproached himself bitterly for having so long refrained from giving her so simple a pleasure.

'Thou's been sorely moped, my love,' I fear,' he said, with a sad kindness.

'Oh, no,' said Arden; 'one can't go out

in the winter, you know, Harry. But now
—oh, do let us go *lots* of expeditions!'

Gerard laughed.

'Farmer Williams thinks of his standing hay!'

Now this was a little too near the truth
to be quite a well-chosen pleasantry.

'I hope, young man,' said Harry
grimly, 'as I think of my wife first.'

'Why, certainly,' said the incorrigible
Gerard; 'don't you see I meant to make a
joke?'

Arden laughed. 'We're always making
jokes,' she said; and 'they're so small no
one else can see them. It takes quite a
long apprenticeship to see the points!'

'Ten years hence,' went on Gerard,
'we shall have you and your brother, Miss
Susie, just as frivolous and inconsequential
as myself; all alike corrupted by this
young woman's unholy influence.'

'It seems odd,' said Susie simply, 'to
think as you've known her so much; longer
than we have, Mr. Rose.'

Harry said nothing, but his face grew set and cold.

Susie was the next to speak. 'Oh, look,' she cried, letting down the window, 'oh, Sylvie, Harry, there it is—there's Stratford! I was at school there, you know, Mr. Rose, when I was a little girl. Oh, Harry, promise me as you'll take me to see Miss Wakefield. 'Twould seem so strange-like not to go. And there's the river; we must row on the river.'

'That's good,' said Gerard; 'and we must go to Shakespeare's house, and see the tomb in the church, and drive to Anne Hathaway's cottage, and give ourselves dyspepsia with three-cornered Stratford cakes.'

'D'you mean Banbury cakes?' said Susie, wondering. 'I never heard ought o' Stratford cakes.'

'Oh, delightful,' cried Arden, clapping her hands; 'Gerard caught tripping! So

you don't know everything at Harvard,
quite? There's just a trifling point or so
of local colour you can pick up better in
Europe, eh, Gerard?'

Strangely enough, though this joke
was very small, no one laughed at it so
heartily as Farmer Williams.

The train stopped, and they got out
and walked down the wide streets of the
bleak little town.

'Well,' said Gerard, as he looked about
him, 'I have often longed to see this place.
It is the Mecca of our drama. I guess,
when the "Mayflower" set out for Ply-
mouth, the Pilgrim fathers little dreamed
that of all the towns in the old country
there would be none for which their
children would cherish so fantastic a devotion as for the birthplace of the Stratford
play-actor. Nothing strikes one so much
in life as the incongruity of things. I call
that an incongruity; they would have
called it a degeneration; Harvard would

call it the influence of culture. To me it's
simply incongruous. There's a delightful
humour about it. And the place itself,
that's incongruous too. There's no breath
of romance here; no comedy-idleness and
sweetness, as there is about Guyscliff, or
Stoneleigh, or Kenilworth. I can see no
reason why Shakespeare should have to be
born in this bare little town. It's just the
one bleak, prose little place in this Elizabethan shire. All the rest is pure *paysage
pour rire*, as Vernon Lee says somewhere,
or Colvin, I don't know. Just the effects
for a stage: low-lying meadows full of
king-cups and lady-smock, the bend of a
full, sleepy river, a plank bridge ; or that
mill at Guyscliff with the balcony for the
stage Princess to come out and sing upon,
and the cascade in front, with the ivied
Hall breaking through the trees. And
Warwick; there's an Ariosto-Fletcher
magic for you! That grey enchanted
castle rising mystically from the grey water

overdrooped with willow-boughs! And, at
the back, hilly streets of mediæval houses
for the retainers to royster and fight in.
There was the place for a playwright to be
born! But here, as I said—I can't allow
why Shakespeare should be born right here.
It gives no stamp, I guess, this place!'

'Hard words break no bones,' said
Harry rather grimly. 'He *wur* born here,
you see, Mr. Rose.'

'I'm so sorry you don't like it!' said
Susie. 'We all think it beautiful—Shakespeare's Stratford.'

'Why, certainly,' cried the young man;
'don't you see that *is* the beauty, Miss
Susie? There's nothing cheap about the
effect! If this town had possessed the
feudal charm of Warwick, or the dreamy
romance of Kenilworth, or the comedy-
picturesqueness of Guyscliff, there would
have been no surprise in Shakespeare
having been born here. But as it is, it's
touching! One thinks the man and the

place intrinsically finer for their being so little in obvious relation to each other. Shakespeare is not the mere product of Stratford, nor Stratford the mere surroundings of Shakespeare. They become valuable entities! One respects the lasting attachment which the greatest poet of all time lavished on these winter-beaten streets. "It hallows him that gives and him that takes." I declare, Miss Susie, I think you are much to be envied, having lived in this town.'

' Oh,' said Susie, rather blankly ; ' I'm glad you like it.'

' Isn't he clever?' cried Arden at the same moment, turning to her husband; but as she turned round she thought she caught an irreverent sentence on his lips. Surely it could not be? What?

' Fine words butter no parsnips '—so it sounded.

' Harry !' she cried; ' are you angry? Why, what's the matter?'

Perhaps if he had told her then, she would have understood in time that he felt himself neglected, but he would not cross her pleasure. He smiled to see her so eager and childish.

'Nay, nay, little maid,' he cried; 'I'm not angered. I meant it for a joke-like, as Muster Rose 'nd say.' A slow grin widened on his face at this shooting of the enemy with his own revolver.

'So glad,' said Gerard, with his fine smile; but he was rather cross. He had let all his theories be disconcerted.

They walked on in silence. 'Where shall we go first?' asked Arden.

'What difference?' said Gerard.

'Only that we must begin somewhere. I suppose a birthplace is as near a beginning as anything can be. Harry, which is the way?'

'Here we are, Sylvie!'

It was indeed the well-known, timbered house. They rang the bell and entered.

' Why, Harry,' said Arden, in a caressing whisper, ' it's not half so pretty as our house at home ! '

' I've allus liked th' old house,' replied her husband in as low a voice; ' but Sylvie, love, I never thought it fit for the likes of thee ! '

' I've been very happy there,' said Arden. And, as they went together through the narrow little house, all Gerard's banter failed to bring a frown to Farmer Williams' serious brow. It was a very happy party that laughed and theorised in the tumbledown brown chambers where Shakespeare played his childhood and dreamed his youth away. They liked to imagine—Arden and Gerard—the many times in which that house had seen him in disgrace ; they invented superior young friends of his, who had doubtless come to see him in the back shop, and were afterwards held up as examples to him by his parents; they fancied the excuses he

would make to slip away to Anne Hathaway in her pretty cottage, and discussed
the attraction which an older woman has
for boys of genius. Gerard had just begun
upon the remonstrances of old Mr. Shakespeare when his good-for-nothing son pro-
posed to join the strolling players, when
Harry interrupted the flow of his would-be
Elizabethan tongue.

'Muster Rose,' he said rather awkwardly, 'I fancy there's a fairish number
o' sights we've got to see.'

'That's so,' said Gerard, comprehending
in one glance the serious faces of Susie and
the attendants. 'It doesn't do to mock
the idol in his temple,' he whispered to
Arden, as he led her out.

She laughed. Harry's face clouded
over again; they were always laughing
together.

They passed the old grammar school
where Shakespeare got his slender schooling, and then they set out for the church,

that stands so well between its broad green
avenue and the sleepy river at the back.
They wandered silently through the aisles,
and looked at the storied tombs with their
rough carving.

'Odd, isn't it?' said Gerard, 'that in
the very years you always call the flower-
ing-time of the Fine Arts in England, your
grandees could get no better tombs carved
for themselves than their great-great grand-
fathers had been accustomed to! What
surface! What paucity of detail! It must
have been a real martyrdom, anyway, for
some travelled courtier and dabbler in Art
to know that when his time came he would
have to repose under the weight of such a
thing as that. Shades of Pisano and Della
Quercia! They all went to Italy, your
lords and scholars. Why in the world did
they never bring some carvers back?'

'We're in church,' interposed Susie
softly; but she was quite as much shocked
at the criticism as the sacrilege. It was all

so fine and rare to her. Gerard bowed, and kept silence till they reached the chancel and the painted bust of Shakespeare.

'Well, I declare,' cried Gerard. 'It's the most pathetic thing I ever saw. Is this all they could do for Shakespeare?'

They stopped and looked at the portrait with interest and wonder; but, after a glance, Arden strayed away. When Gerard lowered his eyes he saw that she had moved forward, and was looking at the nearest monument.

It is indeed a contrast to the rude figure-head which stands for Shakespeare's presence in his church Two young people, in the beautiful, careless dress of the court of Charles II., are looking out of a square carved frame at the passers-by. Handsome youth and beautiful girl, undimmed by age or change, wearing their lace ruffles and bygone finery with an easy grace as out of date as these, they still look out at the altering world with a facile, indifferent interest ; as though, seated in their opera box. they were looking on at a play.

'I like them best,' said Arden, looking up. 'What a difference!' and she glanced back at the painted bust.

'Yes,' answered the young man. 'It's apocalyptic! It brings home to me, with a shock of understanding, the whole social difference between Shakespeare and his London world. The little glover's shop never told us that! But this. Oh, one understands the sonnets now! Let him be what he would. greatest tragedian since Æschylus, greatest comedy-writer of all time, friend and accepted equal of Elizabeth's finest courtiers ; one sees now that he never really was on their level. He was always hopelessly above or below them. He was Shakespeare. He was Shakespeare the glover's son. He lives for all time ; but while he lived on earth he was never the equal of these two beautiful, careless, unrenowned young people.'

'No,' said Arden. 'That's very true.'

'They had the advantage, living, certainly. Look at that vulgar painted face, with its pompous complacency of sitting for its portrait. *Bourgeois* to the end of the finger-tips! And these graceful, facile creatures, with their beautiful manners and unburdened hearts and brains. He might have created such a young fellow as that; he could not become it.'

'Yes,' said Arden again; 'I like them best.'

Harry, who for some time had been listening in growing dudgeon to Gerard's harangue, came forward at this moment. He slipped his hand almost roughly through Arden's arm, and drew her to him.

'Noan the less, my lass,' he said, 'thou's cast in thy lot with th' other side.'

CHAPTER XXVI.

LAUGHING AND CRYING.

It was hot in the hayfield; one of those
days of fierce sudden heat that flit like
tropic birds across the temperate changes
of an English summer. The haymakers
looked flushed and heated, as they wielded
their pitchforks in the striking blazing
sunlight. One woman, who had turned
faint from the heat, was sitting in the
shade on a bank; while Arden—a vision
of coolness in her muslin frock and flap-
ping Siena hat—stooped down to question
her.

'You feel better now?' she inquired.

'Yes, Miss, that I do, Lor' bless you,
Miss; Mum, I ought to say; as asks your

pardon,' said the haymaker, rising as she spoke.

'Do you think you could walk to the house, up the shady path?'

'Lor' yes, Miss. I believe I could.'

'Then go along,' said Arden. 'You ought not to try and work again just yet. I'll set you your dinner in the cool kitchen. You'd better not try dining here with the rest. It's nearly twelve,' she added, looking at her watch.

The haymaker curtsied out her thanks, and walked away.

'*Dio! è cocente!*' cried Arden, as she threw herself down under the tree. 'But I suppose I must even face it.'

She sat for a minute or two quite still, looking at the busy scene.

'And I am dying of heat,' she mused aloud, 'sitting still in the shade in a muslin gown with a sunshade over my head. Poor things, how *can* they do it?'

'This poor thing can't do it any more!'

cried a merry voice, and Gerard, all in white linen, with a pitchfork on his shoulder, sauntered up to her, and threw himself down at her feet. " I'm killed, sire ; and his chief beside, smiling the boy fell dead." ' he quoted, sighing.

' All very fine,' laughed Arden, ' but I don't think much of *your* heroic devotion. Look at Harry.'

' Look at Napoleon!' he cried. ' I never pretended to that ! '

' Well, then, look at me,' said Arden.

' With all the pleasure in life ! I never want to look at anything more " fine-appearing ! " But I can't say I perceive the devotion—much.'

' Gerard !' she cried ; ' and Harry said I had been of so much use.'

' Ornament, I should suggest,' replied the other ; ' that's more in our line, I fancy, Arden. Let me see, was it three swathes of hay that you tossed over, or two. Two, I think.'

'I didn't mean that, you stupid boy! Of course I can't make hay in tight sleeves,' she exclaimed, with triumphant logic.

'Oh, no, of course not,' said Gerard humbly. 'It's so sensible to wear tight sleeves on such occasions ; I might have expected it of you. Of course, you could not work!'

'All very well to laugh! I suppose you were asleep when it happened.'

'What happened?'

'Ah! I shan't say. You were asleep, evidently.'

'I did seem to perceive a piece of melodrama in the distance,' said Gerard musing, 'or perhaps I dreamed it. I appeared to notice a young woman throwing herself upon the prostrate body of a haymaker, and maliciously emptying a mysterious phial down the poor creature's eyes and mouth. She expired soon after in agonies. But I didn't seem to care to allude to the crime in your presence.'

'Gerard!' cried Arden, starting up; 'you horrid boy! Well, I'm going to get her some dinner.'

'The murdered victim?' exclaimed the young man, leaping to his feet in mock alarm. 'Not alone, misguided fair, not alone shalt thou venture into that ghastly presence.'

'Very well,' said Arden, 'come along. I don't think you're much use down here, anyway.'

'Oh, generous praise, not to be answered in words!' cried Gerard. 'My gratitude swells out my heart to silence. But if the devotion of a lifetime——'

'Open the gate!' commanded Arden, laughing. 'I shall think you have got a sunstroke next.'

They went laughing up the rutty lane, made for the carts to travel up and down by. Harry paused in his work to look after them a moment.

'Don't you want to know, Arden?'

said Gera.d at last, after an interval of silence, 'don't you want to know when I am going away?'

'Going away!' Arden stopped still. 'Oh, no; I don't want to know. Don't tell me!' she cried passionately.

Gerard looked at her, surprised.

'You're overtired, dear,' he said, 'with the sun and the walk. Take my arm.'

Neither said anything, till, as they passed through the rickyard, Gerard looked at the two new golden piles.

'Before the last rick is thatched,' he said, 'I shall be gone away.'

Arden raised her eyes. 'I shall be sorry to have you go,' she said.

'And I. Very sorry. We must not lose sight of each other, Arden.'

'No,' she said. 'It's not that I'm afraid of. It's the actual saying good-bye. It kills me saying good-bye! It's like losing things by death; you feel sorry when any one dies, and wish you had done more for

them. I feel like that about parting. Oh.
often I have felt a kind of anguish to leave
a place I have not been very specially
happy in—some holiday place we have
just visited and then left! I was always
miserable to leave. How I used to strain
my eyes to get the last look ; and how I
used to try and fix in my mind just the
way things were arranged in the inn-
parlour ; because I should never see them
again! I always feel that I shall never see
things again. And when one's friends go.
it's like wrenching a piece out of one's life.'

'Yes,' said Gerard ; 'I remember, when
you were a little girl, how miserable you
looked when we went back to Boston. Dear
little Arden, I never forgot your face then.'

'How wretched I was! I've always
had that feeling about letting things go ; it
seems as if nothing else could ever be so
precious. And do you remember Ellie's
telling me to make friends of people
passing through?'

'No,' said the young man. 'How like her!' He laughed softly.

'But I never did, you see,' said Arden. 'You and Ellie, my husband and his sister, are all the friends I have in the world. I have never cared very much for any one else. It will be dreadful to let you go.'

'But I shall come again, Arden, often,' he cried. 'Dear Arden, do you think that out of sight will be out of mind, with me?'

'Oh, I don't know,' she said, impatiently, 'and I don't care. What have I to do with the future? I don't understand it; I can't feel that it's real: it's all blank, dim—ghosts without faces.'

She covered her eyes with her hand, and leaned her arms upon the high gate that led into the yard. After a moment she looked up.

'No, I can dream back the past, but I can't realise meeting again, not even papa.'

'Come in, Arden,' cried the young man,

drawing her by the hand. 'You must come in; you'll be ill.'

They went in to the pretty blossom-coloured parlour, cool and fresh after the heat. 'I can't sit down yet,' said Arden, ' I must go and get the woman her dinner.' She went out, and Gerard, left alone, took down from the wall her well-remembered guitar, and began to thrum on it idly, as he recalled Italy, his childhood, Arden. As he was playing she slipped in behind him, and stood listening in the doorway, till he began to sing, still very softly, some quaint pifferari song, 'Bella Roma—mai lasciar.'

Arden glided forward quietly and suddenly.

'Oh, give it me back,' she cried—'my old life; I was so happy then, so happy. Why did it not last? But it's gone, and it can never come over again—never—never.'

She sank into a chair, crying bitterly.

CHAPTER XXVII.

THE WITNESSES.

HARRY stayed in the hay meadow, working harder than his labourers. He only stopped one moment, to glance at Arden as she flitted out of the field in her fresh white dress, and then he gave a proud sigh. ''Twasn't for naught, as I told the old gen'leman, Sylvie 'ud never break her back o'er the work,' he chuckled to himself as he set to making hay with redoubled energy. It inspired him, in the hot blazing field, with the seed of the hay pricking his eyes, while his back ached and his hard hands blistered with the strenuous tossing and lifting ; it inspirited him and refreshed him to recall that gay sweet vision, white and

cool, whom his labour kept so far from toil.
Only the brightest thoughts visited the
farmer this morning, for looking on the
abundant harvest of the field, with over
the hedge the full-eared corn already turning pale yellow, it was impossible to fancy
anything but prosperity in store.

But perhaps his previous anxieties had
told upon him, perhaps his energy was too
violent, for after a few minutes Harry
staggered and nearly fell. He recovered
his balance and stood leaning on his pitchfork, while the air swam with lights before
his eyes and surged into his ears, something seemed to snap in his brain, and
every moment the sense of being drawn
back into nothingness would recur, but
less forcibly time by time. At last the
farmer was able to stand erect : he tossed
the pitchfork away.

'Neil,' he called, 'I've got a bit of a
stroke, I fear. 'Tis naught, man, naught
to be afeard on. I'll just step up to th'

'ouse and stop work a bit. You'll look
arter the men.'

He walked out of the field, half sorry
to have to leave his labourers, and half
pleased to think of Arden's nursing. How
good she had been to poor Maggie Jones!
It was almost worth while being ill in
the midst of the harvesting, to come in
for her tender kindness, to feel her soft
hands cooling his brow, to hear her
anxious, fearful voice ; at least so Harry
fancied.

He reached the house, and went straight
up to their bedroom, that he might wash
and brush away, as much as might be, the
traces of his illness before showing himself
to Arden. It was characteristic of the
man, that even when he longed for her
sympathy most, he tried to disguise his
illness lest it should frighten her. The
face he saw in the glass looked so purpled
and heavy that it took himself aback.

' It's well,' he muttered, ' as I didn't go

straight in. I should ha' frightened the poor little maid out o' her seven senses.'

There was still a great noise rushing in his ears, so that all sound was uncertain; but Harry thought he recognised the thin notes of the guitar. He imagined Arden sitting alone in the little parlour (for in his confused illness he had forgotten Gerard), sitting alone and suddenly seeing him ill, letting go her instrument and running to wait upon him. The impulse of tenderness that this image awoke was so strong in Harry's heart that he felt he must see her at once. He could not wait to put himself in order ; he would just look from the door that opened on the little stair leading down ; he would only look through the door and glance at her, and retreat before she could see him. His hand was on the knob, and as the door opened the music floated in. Yes, it was the guitar, suddenly, unaccountably it stopped ; and then crying ! Was that a woman's crying ? In his eagerness

Harry stepped out on to the staircase. There beneath him, on the low chair by the hearth, the chair they had chosen together at Warwick, Sylvie was crouched, sobbing desperately. Gerard was kneeling at her side ; he had caught one of her hands ; he was begging her to stop, but she went on crying.

'I was so happy, so happy then ; and it can never come back.'

It was a terrible reaction from his dreams. He felt the blood rushing to his head, and a blind fury coming over him from without, like a cloud. A desire to strike, kill, destroy, that was not anger. For he was, in his inner self, sensible of no violent wrath, only of a terrible despair. She did not love him, then. He had not been able to make her happy. He had ruined her life, hopelessly, beyond restitution. She was crying, and he could not console her. That youth down there might have consoled her ; they loved each other.

All this he dimly felt, while the blood surged and thundered through his veins; while he saw everything turn red, and bright lights beat in his eyes, while a new fierce, strange desire to leap out and murder, awoke in him like an appetite, like the sudden instinct of the tiger tasting blood.

At last he cried out, and Arden lifted her face. How pale she was!

The sight of her awoke the impulse to shield her, which had dominated him so long that it was dominant still, unconsciously, even in this chaos of passion and loss. She must not be frightened, she must not be frightened! The thought came to him as a natural habit, and it saved him from murder.

He came downstairs heavily, slowly, passing by Gerard and taking Arden's hand. She clung to his shoulder with the other arm, crying out that something had happened.

'Ay, ay,' he said, 'summat's happened. Summat as has happened often afore, and 'ull often happen agen ; but it shan't hurt thee. Sylvie, more nor I can help. What was I saying ? '

Again the sense of failing and darkness took him ; he groped for a moment with his hand. It touched Gerard, standing irresolute on the hearth. Harry drew it back, with a swift impulse of loathing.

'You'ld better go, young man,' he said ; 'it's best you keep away. I doan't bear 'ee no ill·will, but I can't rightly stomach the sight of 'ee. Sylvie, is there any one in th' 'ouse ? '

She told him, sobbing with vague fear, that his mother and the servants were in the kitchen, drawing the beer for the men ; and the sick harvester was there also.

'Ay, ay ; call 'em all in,' he said, 'all on 'em as you can find. It's all I can do for you, little 'un ; all I can do. It 'ull show 'em all as I trusted you. But doan't 'ee cry, Sylvie; thou's a young woman, thy life's all to come. Well, well! Tell 'em I'm in the brown parlour. I'll be there as soon as any. It's all I can do,' he muttered to himself, as he staggered heavily across the passage. 'Poor little maid, I can't set her free and I can't make her love me. I can but trusten her.'

He stooped down when he had reached the other room, looking for something in the old bureau where he kept his ledgers, and when he raised himself with the parchment in his hand he saw Sylvie, his stepmother, and three or four of the Farm servants huddled together in the doorway. Mrs. Williams sprang forward, but he put her aside with a gentle authority not to be denied. His face looked very grey, and his voice was weak and thick. The group in the doorway looked at him for orders: they had a confused notion that he meant to stop the harvest.

'Sit ye down,' said Harry at last, 'sit

ye down over there and listen. I'm a going to read you my will. Curtis, Kingston, Swinburne, here, you witness as I sign my name—and now listen, all on you— Mrs. Jones and all—ay Neil, there you are. You're the witnesses.'

He stopped a moment; no one dared to speak, but Arden gave him one swift appealing glance. She could not understand what it all meant, it was all a dreadful, clueless mystery. 'Nay, Sylvie,' he said, 'doan't 'ee cross me. I'm that moithered I can't rightly think. . . . I got it done the day th' insurance officer refused me. Well, I'm glad on it now, glad on it now . . . .'

His voice died away, and he remained for a moment silent, his face vague and almost meaningless, a dazed look in his bloodshot eyes; but the silence remained unbroken. Arden had fainted unnoticed.

'Yes,' he went on, speaking as if to himself, 'I got it done when we wur in Leam-

ington together. And th' insurance officer
refused my life—a bald, fattish man with
a blear eye, he wur. I niver liked the
looks of him. But I thought: "Well, old
chap, say what you like, it shan't make
any difference to her; she shan't be any
the wuss for it, I can tell you, the poor
little maid." '

A smile played over his lips. He
seemed to forget his hearers.

' And yet,' he went on, ' I never thought
o' proving it. I might ha' dropped down
sudden and left her with her thirds, as
if I'ld no call to make it good to her. But
it's all signed fair and clear, all fair and
clear, afore the witnesses.'

The words seemed to rouse him from
his retrospect.

· You're the witnesses, remember,' thundered Harry, ' and, as you look for the
kingdom of Heaven, I charge you all that
you allus say and swear that this is my
true will and testament. And if so be's

the Devil and the powers of them below should ever lead me away to sign aught different it's to be o' no account, them other wills. Doan't you think it binding, if ever I be so led away as to say aught agen a second marriage. I *might* go mad. I feel it,' said Harry softly; 'there's such a spinning and roiling in my head as though I were Raynham mill-wheel churning the water, turning and turning for ever.' He put up his hand to his head for a moment, with the pathetic wonder of a strong man suddenly ill. 'But I'm sound enough now,' he went on— 'sane in mind and body, as the dockment runs.'

Mrs. Williams had started to her feet at the mention of the pain in Harry's head. She only waited for his voice to stop to break out into wailing lamentations.

'Oh, th' arrow leaves!' she began, 'where's Susie put the powdered yarrow leaves? I allus keep 'em all ground up and handy, these ten years and more ; and now, now, she's got the key down in the hayfield.'

'Nay, mother,' said Harry, 'sit ye down. There 'll be time enough for talking and doctoring arter.'

He took the opened parchment in his hand and rose to his feet, as if in reverence of the occasion. The servants rose too, and Mrs. Williams, who was sobbing loudly with her handkerchief pressed to her eyes ; but Arden, scarcely recovered from her faint, lay back unmoved and almost insensible. It did not seem to touch her, this strange and fearful scene, or to be more real than the memory of dreams that haunt us on the brink of waking. She lay back wearily, as if suffering it to have its way.

'This is my last will and testament,' began the farmer, in a sing-song drawling voice, quite unlike his passionate utterance, 'written this second day o' December,

I being then sound and sane o' mind
and body, in the Bath Hotel at Leamington.

'Whereby I leave to my dear and
much-loved sister, Susan Williams, the
cottage in Wood Lane with the garden
appertaining, and the three cottages known
as Ford End with all lands and appertan-
ences thereto ; and these I leave her with
my love.

'And I leave my stepmother, Sarianna
Williams, th' interest of five hundred
pounds Consols for the term of her natural
life, the same being half of the fortune
left me by my mother Margaret Williams,
in her own right, which I bequeath now to
her that has been a second mother to me,
the same to go at decease of th' aforesaid
Sarianna Williams to th' aforesaid Susan.
And I bequeath the aforesaid Sarianna the
cottages at th' end of th' orchard, for the
term of her natural life, to descend there-
after to the aforesaid Susan.'

'Oh, Harry!' sobbed Mrs. Williams, but she dared say no more.

'And all the rest of my land, property, furniture, and estate in whativer kind, the two hunderd acre o' land with the 'ouse and buildings appertaining known as Williams' Farm, the land and 'ouse in Preston parish known as th' Apple Tree Farm, the five hundred pound Consols being the other moiety of my mother's private fortin and the seven hundred pound in Warwick Bank I leave, in testimony of the perfect trust and love I bear her, to the absolute disposal and control of my dearly beloved and honoured wife—my dearly beloved wife—Sylvie!'

The husky sing-song tones were suddenly broken through by a choking cry.

'Sylvie!' he called again; but, as she rose, he did not look at her or seem to see her, staring round wildly with bloodshot, eyes.

'It's come,' he cried at last. 'Thou's

free, Sylvie.' He fell heavily to one side, like a tree cut through at a stroke, his head striking against the corner of the settle with a heavy sound. He did not move; he did not even groan, but lay just as he had fallen on the floor.

Arden sprang forward, dazed, aghast. She flung herself down upon the floor, peering into the dead man's face, kissing his hands, calling on him wildly.

'Harry, Harry,' she kept on crying and calling, 'look at me, speak to me only, dear Harry! I can't live without you. Oh, my husband, my love; I can't let you go, Harry! Oh, God! he doesn't understand!'

Alas! No. It was too late; he would never understand. The one word that might have saved him could never reach his palsied brain. He had died for the want of it, and now he could not hear.

But all through the afternoon and through the night, long after the doctor had pronounced the last fluttering, impotent breath of life extinct, Arden sat upstairs, dry-eyed, in a still chamber, with her dead husband's head lying in her lap. She did not weep ; but every now and then the air was rent with a sighing, gasping cry ; and every now and then those who passed outside the closed door would hear her calling frantically on the deaf, unconscious man, who had never denied her slightest wish before, who would not hear her now, though she broke her heart with calling.

And side by side downstairs two other women crouched, weeping bitterly, and shuddering afresh at every echo of her cries.

CHAPTER XXVIII.

AFTERWARDS.

THE harvest was all gathered in, the harvest that no master surveyed with pride. The house was quiet and desolate, there would be that year no merry-making. The master was dead and in his grave. Two women, clad in crape and very pale, occupied the blossom-coloured bridal parlour.

'And you will not stay and help me?' Arden was saying. She looked ill, but there was no fear now that she would lose her reason or her life. Horror, not grief, had threatened to turn her brain, and the horror was past. She had grown familiar with the cold, holy look on Harry's face. It only spoke to her now of love and loss.

'I can't, Sylvie,' said her stepmother-in-law. 'I'm sorry for you enough, poor child, goodness knows. I wish I could have been of more assistance. But there's Susie to think of first.'

'Yes,' said Arden. He was dead who had given his first thoughts to her.

'Dr. Grant's quite positive,' went on Mrs. Williams, 'as she'll recover if I take her away at once. He says he knows a lady at Warwick who was quite as wasted, and she recovered. She must stay at least a year, he says, and we're to travel about as much as may be, so as to keep her mind off it. I don't know how we could have afforded it, but for you, Sylvie.'

'Poor Susie,' sighed the widow, 'poor, poor Susie!'

'I wish she'd consent to see you, Sylvie,' went on the other. ''Tisn't my fault; but, poor child, she is not answerable for her actions. She keeps crying out against you ; it's terrible to sit by and listen.'

Arden shuddered.

' There, there,' cried Mrs. Williams, ' you mustn't take it so to heart. She don't know what she's saying, poor child. But you mustn't fret if I can't make her see you, Sylvie. I daren't so much as speak of you before her, even to tell her of the deed of gift.'

' There is no need,' said Arden, in the same colourless, unvarying voice. ' I would rather you did not tell her now. When she gets well you shall tell her, and she will be glad to come back to the old place. I shall be gone then.'

' And what will you do with yourself, Sylvie?' asked the little old woman, kindly.

' I shall go back to Rome,' said Arden ; ' I would like to do some good with Harry's money, but I don't know how. I shall paint, I think : I shall find something to do.'

'Yes,' said Mrs. Williams. 'But I meant about the property.'

'The lawyer tells me the tenants are all right. There's nothing here for me to see after It's for you, now, to see after a tenant for the farm. It's Susie's now. As for me, I had better go home; I don't understand this country.'

'Ah, poor child,' said the other; 'you'd best get back to your own ways and your own friends. You're not fit to rough it among the likes of farmers and such like.'

'No,' said Arden, quietly. 'I don't think I am fit to live.'

'Poor child, poor child!' repeated the older woman tenderly, smoothing the little hand that lay on the window ledge. 'I'm sure I wish I was free to give my mind to nursing you up.'

'You have been very kind,' said Arden, and she bent down and kissed the wrinkled prettiness of Mrs. Williams' face. 'I think you saved my life; and you might have hated me, like Susie.'

'La, Sylvie!' cried the older woman; but Arden had gone, had drifted away from her side.

It was now a month since the farmer had fallen down dead, so suddenly, never to move again. Susie had nearly died of grief: of silent, overmastering grief; and now there was but a hope of life. She was young, she might recover, but the shock of her brother's death had terribly shaken her in mind and body. Her love for Harry was as old as her life, it had been the very mainspring of her life; and now he was dead. As the conviction of his jealousy forced itself upon her mind she had grown to hate the frail slight nature which had, unwittingly, goaded him to death. She could not bear to hear any one speak of Arden. The poor young widow would have been terribly desolate but for kind little Mrs. Williams, who, forced for the first time in her life to take the lead in an emergency, surprised no one more than herself by her skill and courage. Everything had been left to her; all the arrangements. So that when Arden left her she had no time to sit and muse on cruel destiny, like the young widow upstairs. She went to finish the necessary packing.

They were to start for Normandy next day, she and Susie. The one hope of saving the girl lay in change; they were to start as soon as possible, and there was much to be done first. Not the least difficult of the tasks which the little old lady had set herself, was the persuading Susie to say good-bye to her sister-in law.

It was long before she succeeded. But at last, in the morning, when their boxes were being heaped upon the waggon, Susie gave in. Mrs. Williams ran to summon Arden, who was haunting the corridor like a lonely ghost. 'Come in, Sylvie,' she cried, with

a gleam of brightness in her tear-swollen
eyes. Arden entered.

Susie was seated on the foot of the
bed, dressed all ready for her journey.
There was a terrible alteration in her
face, her features looked large and stern,
now that the flesh had fallen away from
her cheeks, and her blue eyes were hollow
and large, with an implacable glitter in
them.

' Susie!' cried the other girl, falling on
her knees by her side.

' Get up,' said Susie, sternly.

Arden obeyed. She stood looking at
her sister-in-law; she forgot to think of
herself, she was so sorry for her.

' Can you forgive me, Susie?' she said
at last.

Susie did not answer.

' Oh, Susie, Susie!' cried Arden, terri-
fied at a resentment incomprehensible to
her. ' You can't go away like this and
leave me. We may never see each other

again; and I, too, am miserable. I've lost him, too. Look at me kindly once, Susie, for good-bye; you're *his* sister.'

' Yes,' said Susie; 'good-bye.'

She held out her hand, but not willingly; rather as if she would accomplish a promised hateful task. Arden seized the little hand and stood holding it.

' Why won't you look at me, Susie?' she said. ' It was not my fault, God knows.'

' It was not your fault, I suppose !' said Susie, looking at the weeping girl with severe unpardoning eyes; ' it was not your fault, but it was your nature; and I shall never forgive you.'

Arden looked at her a moment, but she saw it was hopeless to plead. Besides, she thought Susie under a delusion, and dared not cross her deranged fancy. ' Good-bye, my dear little sister,' she said, very sadly, and loosed her clasp. Then she turned away, and left the girl alone with her mother.

Arden had no mother to console her. She went into her little white parlour, bare now, and stripped of her treasures, for the new tenant was coming in within a week. She sat by the window and looked drearily out, while Curtis and Neil placed the old-fashioned luggage on the waggon. Then the trap came round, and Susie, closely veiled, got in. Mrs. Williams ran into the parlour, and kissed Arden. ' Good-bye, my other daughter ! ' she cried ; then she, too, got into the spring-cart, and they drove away, leaving Arden alone behind. She sat there till dinner-time, when she could not eat ; but afterwards she went upstairs, and began, wearily enough, to drag out her boxes and fold her clothes.

It was growing dusk when she heard a voice in the hall ; it was Mrs. Lawrance's voice. She ran down, glad of the familiar sound.

'Come in, come in,' she cried; 'I am so glad you are come!'

'Oh, Sylvie!' cried the elder woman, 'I'm sure I've intended coming every minute, but your grandpa's that ill I couldn't bring my mind to leave 'im: and this marning, when I heard as they'd left you alone, I sent over for Mrs. Willis to come and keep 'im company, so's I might come round and see you.'

'Thank you,' said Arden, sitting down on the red-covered bench by her visitor's side. 'It was good and kind of you to come. I'm sorry grandpapa is ill.'

'Oh, Sylvie,' said Mrs. Lawrance, beginning to cry, 'most likely 'tis sent as a judgment upon me, as couldn't endure to be out of his thärts, so jealous and exacting as I was! Oh, the judgments of God are terrible hard to bear! I foller him about day and night, up and down the stairs, traipsing in and out of all the rooms; I never dare to leave him a moment; and yet he don't appear to reckernise me.'

'Who?' said Arden. 'What is it? What new trouble?'

'You may well say that,' sobbed Mrs. Lawrance. 'Oh, I mind me so well how he was accustomed to say they never came single. So clever and infarmed as he allus was. And now, now——'

'Tell me,' said Arden, softly; 'don't cry; let me help you, if I can.'

'You're a good child,' said the elder woman, gratefully. 'But I don't rightly know how to explain it, Sylvie. He's been terrible shakey all this 'car; I've often told yer so. And the shock o' Williams' misfortin was too much for him. We're both in the same boat, Sylvie, you and I.'

'What,' cried Arden, 'is he dead?'

'Not in his corporal state; but his mind's dead, Sylvie, his mind's dead. He as allus was so clever, too! He's

forgotten me, and aül the time we've
lived together. He rambles aül over the
'ouse, looking for your father, child.
Door after door, he opens them, and
"John!" he calls; and then, when the
room's empty, as it allus is, he turns
round to me, and says, "Mrs. Warner,"
he says, as you know was my name afore
he married me, " I think my son must
have gone out."'

'It's dreadful!' said Arden, horror-
struck.

'So it is, child, so it is. And aül day
long, it's the self-same weary search, over
and over again, in aül the rooms, and it's
allus John, he wants, or his first wife.
And if I make so bold as to touch his
sleeve, and say, "Won't you sit down a
bit, dear?" he turns quite sharply round,
and speaks to me as if I was a stranger.'

'I am sorry from my heart,' cried
Arden. 'Poor Mrs. Lawrance!'

'Yes, Sylvie,' went on the elder

woman. 'I've aften and aften felt repentant as I didn't love you better; but I was so swallowed up in your grandpa'; I never thaüt of anything but 'im. And now I'm gone clean out of his mind. I'm no more use to him than any other woman—only to keep him out o' the way o' the furniture, and see as he don't stumble on the stairs.'

She could not speak for a minute; then she went on again in a weak, broken voice—

'At last, I'm put to it so, I've come to ask your assistance, Sylvie. I'm fair exhausted, traipsing early and late; and it flashed across me, as, may be, you'd come and help nurse; you being homeless-like yourself, with your husband dead; and in trouble, so jealous as he was.'

'Jealous!' cried Arden, starting to her feet, her eyes flashing. 'Do they say that—jealous? But they don't know,' she went on, in a softer tone; 'no one can

know, but I, how good, and generous,
and noble he was, my Harry!' She
stood for a moment, her hands clasped,
looking before her with shining eyes.
Then she came up to the elder woman,
who was still sitting on the ottoman, and
still crying. 'Come, Mrs. Lawrance,' she
said, 'take me home with you. Let us
try together if we cannot help poor grandpapa.'

EPILOGUE.

It was a warm spring morning at the Bushes. Mrs. Lawrance was standing in the porch speaking earnestly to Gerard Rose.

'I'm none so disconcerted as she was out, Mr. Rose,' she was saying, 'since it's affarded me th' opportunity of putting in a word. I'm sure you've my best wishes, if they'll do you any good. T'was allus my opinion as you'ld have made her a better 'usband than that poor hot-tempered Harry Williams, as she worships like a saint.'

'Does she?' said Gerard eagerly, a little surprised.

'La, yes. She never seems to so much

as think of anything without a reference to
what e'ld ha' thaüt of it. But, as I was
saying, you're much more fitted for Sylvie
than the likes of he—though it 'ull be bitter
to spare the child—she's the sunshine of
the place, I allus say.'

'She was always so sweet and gay,' said
Gerard.

'*I* remember when she was very different,' said Mrs. Lawrance ; 'but now she's
so considerate and has such a way with her
as her poor granpa 'ull do anything for her,
though he allus calls her by her mother's
name.'

'Indeed ; and where shall I find her ?'
asked Gerard.

'Most likely she'll be coming over the
fields from the churchyard. She's been to
lay some vi'lets on Williams' grave. She'll
be coming back by now, for dinner's at 'alf-
past one,' said Mrs. Lawrance, pulling out
her watch.

Gerard took his leave and walked towards the fields. He had got as far as the canal bridge, where he had stood with Arden two years ago, where he had first heard of her marriage, when he saw her in front of him coming down the hill. She did not see him, for her eyes were looking far away beyond the horizon; a very sweet and patient gentleness was in her face and bearing. When she came near the bridge, she saw him standing near her.

'Gerard!' she said, without any surprise.

'Yes, Arden, I came to see you. I want to know if you are well and happy.'

'Oh, yes!' said Arden softly, 'I am waiting in peace.'

Gerard looked at her with a certain exasperation. He would rather she had been less calm, less contented. Still he felt awed by her aloofness.

'I am happy now,' she went on, 'for I have been sitting by Harry's grave. I always feel so quiet there, so sure of meeting

him again. It is just such a day to-day
as it was the spring before last, when
he took me to Farley. Ah, you were not
there.'

'No,' said Gerard; 'but are you going
to live here, Arden, in this village?'

'I don't know,' she said. 'Grandpapa
wants me now. I am able to be of some
use. And soon my sister and her mother
will be coming home. Susie wrote to me
yesterday.'

'Don't you ever look back?' cried
Gerard, a little impatiently; 'don't you
regret the old life? Don't you wish ever
to come back to Italy—to Rome?'

'Yes,' said Arden, 'I look back. I
think how much happier I ought to have
been. I think how discontented I was with
my happiness. And I try and learn to be
content and patient, and to care for other
people, like Harry.'

The tears had risen to her eyes; she
looked dreamily away.

'You never understood him, Gerard,' she said. 'No. I don't want to go back to Italy, I think; not for always. I should feel so far away from him there; he never went there. But this was his home; he always lived here. And the places he has left me belonged to him, and I can do all the things for him that he meant to have done; and the people all knew him. They lived on his land and took his wage, and I belong to him too, more here than anywhere else. He never seems very far off from me —Harry!'

Gerald looked at her for a moment. Yes, there was something unreal in the sweet passion that lit up her face. Yet none the less she looked happy; and stronger, too, than she had seemed two years ago. Then he held out his hand.

'Good-bye, dear,' he said; 'I cannot stay any longer now.'

'Good-bye,' said Arden. She did not ask him to stay.

Something fell out of her dress as she moved her arm. Gerard stooped and picked it up for her. It was a little bunch of the violets she had laid upon her husband's grave.

THE END.

www.ingramcontent.com/pod-product-compliance
Lightning Source LLC
Chambersburg PA
CBHW020100030726
47498CB00006B/1870